THE

FLANEUR

THE

FLANEUR

WRITTEN BY

GIULIANO GIOVANNI

First Printing: 2019

Hardcover Edition: 2021

ISBN: 978-0-578-95375-5

Giuliano Giovanni
269 S. Beverly Drive #901
Beverly Hills, CA 90212-3807

www.theflaneurbook.com

flâneur [flä'nər]- an idler, loafer, or lounger.

A French word borrowed from the old Norse verb *flana* which means “to wander without purpose".

Contents

PROLOGUE

What an orchestra! The café! I close my eyes to hear the voice of the void! She speaks to me as if she is a nymph and I her king. Enough poetry! I will spare you of my pseudo-intellect. I will bring a halt to my exalted cries of antiquity! We can do away with these superfluous allegories! Art does not come from the ancients! Art is all around me! It comes in the form of patrons of this fine café! Their obscure conversations are fine-tuned in stochastic beauty. Adagio to allegro! The café is a dance more seductive than Salome. The ensemble of various walks of life form the ultimate disquiet. When I am a forgotten sphinx in the corner of the room, unwatched by would-be sophists conversing about everything, all the while I say nothing to no one, that iota of time I am the happiest and most alive! Choosing not to say anything is my favorite choice. Besides, tea and coffee are much better conservationists than I; they attract customers to spend their time, money, and above all their ego at this café. Oh! The ego spent at cafes around the world! Ego is the most invaluable currency of humanity. Revolutions to banal chatter, euphoric rendezvous to scientific breakthroughs, philosophical speculations to rash ignorant actions; all are pure sentiments that begin at cafes.

You may ask me, “What separates you from the rest of humanity in cafes?”. I am a flâneur, which is just a synonym for a café historian or nosy observer. There are several traits one must possess to be a flâneur: you must be talented at not being talented, an urban recluse, a polyglot that speaks only in incomprehensible languages, a tea mongering night-dreamer, a lover of humans but an abhorrer of social interactions past hello, and someone with more to write than to say. If you encompass all these traits, then you are a true flâneur. If you are someone that spends more time telling others of the books you are writing, the secrets you possess, talents you allegedly have, or your insipid achievements, then you are most likely an anti-flâneur. The modern terminology would be someone trying to be "hip" or look like they have attained some sort of societal enlightenment. Authentic flâneuring is a hard lifestyle. We apes are hardwired to speak and not to think, always showing off our rocks and sticks of pabulum. Flâneuring is an existential fight against millions of years of evolution. This to me is powerful. Names and social ranks mean a lot to apedom, shedding those prehistoric habits is a feat in-itself; to be un-irked by being ignored by others is admirable. However, one must not confuse being an outcast with flâneuring. The last refuge of an outcast is usually a cafe, but you can differentiate the outcasts from the flâneur by how loud and odious they are. To further clarify, flâneuring is not an alternative for failing at being social; it is a lifestyle of a modern epicurean.

There is a myriad of pleasures of being a flâneur, yet the best part is the free show of deductive and inductive observation that unfolds in front of you. One must undress human behavior; at the same time, one must hear the unheard, see the unseen, and feel the unfelt. Our senses are unreliable, so we should perceive our surroundings in reverse, making use out of our frail faculties, this way we can live a life in-between deduction and induction, never trusting nor distrusting.

Now with the foreground set, we can begin on the subject I wish to convey to you the reader: the lives of people I have observed in cafes. None are worth merit, yet here I am wasting ink to write about them. My job as a café historian is to give an abstract recollection of my eavesdroppings; I must tell tales that have no author. This all probably sounds extremely pretentious to you, because to a degree it is. My own vanity compels me to live a life of hedonism for the nonsensical, which ultimately led me to write this senseless collection of stories.

This book has no goal or intrinsic meaning. You can shut this book right now forever, or read it 10 times, read it backwards while riding your bike (though I would not recommend it), read every chapter out of order, eat every 7th page, give it to a co-worker you hate as a gift, use it as toilet paper, or marry it (most likely you can find at least one place where you can legally marry an object), you may detest it, fall in love with it, or forget it all together. Either way it matters not to me. The only advice I give to the reader is not to take anything I just said seriously. The same goes for these little tales of idiosyncratic stupidity. Lastly, don't read this like a book: say it like a pointless conversation.

A SHIFT

A hodgepodge of voices coming from a large table of well-to-doers sullied the concentration of one of the waiters. He tripped on the leg of a pulled-out chair and dropped his tray of sugar. His manager Ballio, muscular, short, and about 60 years of age, came running over to him and grumbled, "You really should pay attention. If you are going to last here, you must pay attention to the chairs. Their odd shape can cause you to trip. You are lucky you weren't carrying anything expensive." The young waiter apologized to his manager and went back to his duties. The café was closing early that day, it was a Sunday before a holiday.

Ballio seemed more magnanimous than usual. He went to every table to see if anyone needed anything. This was unlike him though; he never was a people-pleaser.

The young waiter loaded four plates on to his tray. On Sundays the veteran food expediter was off, the young waiter was out of luck and would have to absorb the carrying capacity. Strutting along with overconfidence, he again forgot to mind the precarious chair jutting outwards. With double the ferocity this time around, he tripped again. A vectoring kaleidoscope of airborne tea cakes, banana cream pies, and tiramisus landed on the table of same pedantics that initially distracted him. Ballio rushed over to the scene of mush. The gaggle of narcissists demanded reparations for the mess. "You should fire this sorry excuse of a waiter! This is the worst service I have ever had! You have stained my new blazer! Do know how much this jacket is worth? Probably more than your rent you idiot! Are you going to pay for my jacket? Oh—wait—you can't because you're a waiter! You better give us a refund, or I will tell my friend at the food magazine about my experience here" said demandingly the leader of café tyrants. Ballio refunded them reluctantly. The group slimed out in the same grotesque way they came in. The young waiter was at the register having a small panic attack. "This can't be happening on my first day, this job isn't for me. I won't last the week or even the day." he said to himself unaware if anyone was listening. From across the room, he looked slightly insane. His hands were shaking so much you could have sworn he had some sort of prion disease. Ballio, looking annoyed, came to confront the young waiter.

"Did you really have to make things more difficult for me today? Did you? I would usually fire or write someone up for that kind of negligence, but I am not in the mood to be moody. Not on my last day. I have worked here for most of my life. This shift is something I have been looking forward to for longer than you have been alive. I could care less if you stay, get fired, or quit. Don't agitate yourself with thinking I am going to do something. It's almost time to close. Come help me clean up your mess. Go get the mop!" ordered Ballio in an uncaring tone. The splattered cake on the floor had changed in hue. The color palate mixed into a Mandelbrot-like swirl of decadence. North of a hundred dollars of dessert had been wasted. This mess brought a weird sense of nostalgia to Ballio. He remembered all the times he had cleaned up such catastrophes. It was peculiar that he was not rushing to finish. All those years he rushed his coworkers and underlings to clean as quickly as possible, yet his present low speed seemed alien to him. Ballio was a man of prudence and rapidity, not a man of leisure. Slowing down to this pace triggered his axons to fire in an odd fashion. It was the first occasion he took his time with his job, and since his job was his life, the first time in his life as well.

Ballio looked at the chair beside him. Did he dare break his own rule? To sit down on the clock was a pet peeve of his. While the newcomer was mopping, Ballio decide to sit down. The young waiter was too preoccupied with mopping to notice him sitting at the table. Ballio glanced at every object in the room. Every object he could deconstruct. Every inch was for-itself. Every signal speck moved like a self-aware cog. They all turned so he could see the grand machine that was the café. Each part had its own autonomy but was also a part of a collective. Even the staff members seemed vital. Before this realization he looked at them as means to an end, now they seemed integral to the survival of the cafe. An oddity had elucidated inside him. The plates, napkins, cups, mugs, and silverware started to sing a somber death hymn:

Many have used us,
Many have broken us,
Many have discarded us,
Yet we gave everyone everything!

Every walk of life have consumed off our brow,
Taken food and drink of mirth,
Paid innumerable tax to gorge themselves,
Pleasured their tongues by using us as tools!

Lo, ye Ballio! Our trusted general that always cared for us when no one did!
All the late nights you stayed overtime to make sure we were clean!
All the early mornings you woke up and presented us to the world!

How many guests have we served under your rule?
How many stomachs were satiated by our help?
How much dirty money was spent just to use our bodies as caveats for pleasure?

Why, our general, do you leave us after all this time?
This boy you train will not last nor the next one!
No employee will show us such benevolence!
You mustn't leave us!

Ballio laughed as they pleaded. He knew his time was up. As bittersweet as these anthropomorphized objects sounded, nothing would convince him to stay. However, a sense of angst came over Ballio with the understanding of his near departure. His whole life was the café; without it, what would he do? A retirement package was granted to him, yet what would he spend the rest of his life doing? Other questions jumped up even more detrimental to his ego than the aforementioned: Why did he waste his life working in this café? What compelled him to work here all these years? Surely, he could have done something else with his life. A monsoon of regret submerged him.

Poor Ballio felt the urge to do something monotonous to distract his mind from imploding. The register hadn't been closed out, he counted the money in a staccato pace, stopping at intervals of reflection, then quelling those regretful thoughts to resume counting. The young waiter, who was a virgin to any job, struggled to finish cleaning the immense cake spill. From the motion of his moping, you could tell this was the first time in his life he had mopped. The boy, I presumed, was the product of a sheltered childhood with a mother that did anything for him and a father that bought everything for him. He had a pathological need to be validated by his parents, having a job would make them somewhat happy for him; he could show them that he was responsible. Even though it was the last time he would see Ballio, he was utterly afraid of him. Ballio was an omen of a man that he did not want to become, a bitter nobody at a dead-end job. Never had he encountered a man that gave him such a vehement insecurity as Ballio did.

The young waiter was incapable of pondering his own pusillanimity, cowardice was programmed as his failsafe; he had misplaced hope that Ballio would take pity on him and be gregarious. “This mop isn’t soaking up the cake. What would be a better way for me to clean it?” the young waiter asked vulnerably. Ballio looked up at the boy and gave him a look that would instill fear into any laymen of his craft. “You made me lose my count. Did your parents ever teach you how to clean? There is a rag in the bucket over there! You’re going to have to scrub the floor instead. I am done in twenty minutes. Please be done before then. I don’t want the openers tomorrow to be left with your mess!” whinged Ballio.

Ballio moved on to the end-of-day deposits and paperwork. Every task he kept rehashing to himself that it was the last time he would perform it; the soon to be retired funambulist was in the death throw of his final tightrope walk. Ten minutes went by, and the young waiter had miraculously finished cleaning up. To Ballio’s amazement, the room looked slightly better than he had anticipated. Now they had ten awkward minutes to kill before clocking out.

They sat down at the same malaprop table from before. The young waiter, trying to avoid talking, looked at his watch and fiddled with the hour hand. Ballio sensed the boy’s uneasiness and realized he had been a bit harsh on him. The young waiter tried to think of something to ask Ballio. Before he could scavenge for something to say, Ballio beat him to the punch. “You did a decent job cleaning up for your first day. You might be able to appease the owners. Keep up the good work.” remarked Ballio empathically. The boy was surprised that Ballio gave him a compliment. “Thanks— Thanks for being so patient with me. It must be tiresome putting up with new trainees. I appreciate you not firing me today. If you don’t mind me asking though—what made you quit? You have worked here for a while, and you are the best worker the café has. Why quit now?” asked the young waiter with a little more confidence. Ballio was taken aback by the boy’s frank question. Most newcomers would hold their tongues instead of being this forward. “I just had enough. I wanted to quit before I resented the café. Quitting while I am ahead would be an apt maxim to describe my actions. Plateauing as a café manager is far from enjoyable. What made you want to have this as your first job?" he retorted. "This was the only place in town that would hire someone with zero experience. My family wanted me to try my luck without their help. I could have gone to work for their business, but they insisted I should get my feet wet in the real world first—so here I am. Hopefully I don't have to do jobs like this for too long. I just started college and one day I will have a job that will make me appreciate my past work. Soon I will work for my family's company as a learned man…" said the young waiter with an air of benign arrogance.

This kind of naivete irritated Ballio. The boy kept talking and talking. Blabbering and blabbering. Ballio looked at the clocked, only five minutes had elapsed and still five to go. He couldn't stand to hear this verbal lesion leaking idiotic bile any longer.

"Listen kid, I know you mean well, but you have to stop talking and let me give you some perspective. Everything you did today was a first in your life. Your first training session, order taking, and big mess-up. Picture this: You will never do these things as your first time again. From now onwards you will live your life oblivious of this principle. Then in 40 years from now, when you look back on your mistakes, you will remember this day very clearly since it was your first day on the battlefield. Yet, every day afterwards will become hazy. Days will become months that will become years that will become decades. It will be the same anywhere you go. At every new job you will do things for the first time, and you will gloat with that same arrogant tone. Your arrogance is the submit of your ignorance. I would advise you to appreciate not just the first things you do in a job, but everything in-between the beginning and the end. Look at all these tables, think of all the people that will tip you badly, spit on you, complain about you, reject your kindness. One day you will see a group of pretty girls or handsome guys that you will try to make a move on. They will reject you because you are a waiter: a peasant wearing a white dress shirt."

"I like to think of these tables as an allegory to what life will throw at you. The tables are empty now, but tomorrow they will be filled with problems that take the form as impatient patrons. It won't be all bad though. Some of these tables you may meet those who take pity on us, those who desire to converse with us, those homely-looking people that have a proclivity for waiters and are romanced by our lower-class novelty. You may even meet your future wife or husband in this café. Or you get fired tomorrow! Find a new job! The process repeats itself!"

"One thing is for certain—at least here (unlike retail) people will not ignore you. Until we are replaced with machines, customers always want your attention. What they will ignore is that you are human. They will look at you like a stone carving stuck out of time. It is hard for a customer to see us as humans and not as order-taking automatons hell bent on pleasing them. Be prepared for abysmal peer to peer interaction. Kids that make even your family look poor will laugh and gawk. 'Look! It's what his name! I went to high school with him! Look what he does now!' they will say. Their entourage will parrot them, while you want to vomit with hatred and embarrassment in your gut. This is the life of the working class. Your family did not raise you to be one of us, they want you to get a taste of lower class to scare you from never becoming it. You won't last very long in the workforce. You know why? You'll always have some family cash to fall back on. Stop lying to yourself and me. You and I both know the real reason you're here. It is to show mommy your little tap dance and above all to lie to yourself that you are a hard worker, when really you are a spoiled kid. You are not cut out for this. I can see it in your eyes. You have the eyes of boy that has seen too little. Never experiencing hardship is dangerous. When real issues arise, you will lack the ability to cope with them. I am the face of the life that is not easy, you may not agree with me, but you know I am right".

The speech went on deaf ears. The boy was not only deeply offended by these statements but was viscerally disturbed by Ballio's perspective. Obviously, the picture Ballio had painted was autobiographical, yet the boy sank into his chair and looked at his watch again, trying just as he did before not to have a connection.

Ballio looked at the clock. "Two minutes. Do you have anything to say kid before I go for good?". He had nothing to say. He just wanted Ballio to leave. The last hundred and twenty seconds were rushing downstream towards the waterfall of everlasting resignation. Finally! Thirty seconds left. Ballio made his way to the punch card station. Ten seconds, five seconds, one second. Ballio punched his card and left it on the counter.

Clearing out his locker, a feeling of *ataraxia* came over him; he could live the life he always wanted, unbounded by the workday.[1] On his way out, he noticed the young waiter still sitting at the table in a daze. Ballio felt like he should say something, maybe one last adieu before he left for good. Looking at the young and frazzled waiter, he remembered his fist day all those distant years ago, it wasn't so different than the boy's. He knew the speech wasn't for the young waiter, it was for him and his ego alone. A sirocco of solace blew over him when he gave that euphoric speech. It didn't matter that the boy didn't fully listen. The boy had nothing to do with his years of hardship. Ballio, without even saying goodbye to the boy or the place that he spent most of his life, exited the café. He didn't think to look back, that speech was his final goodbye.

The boy gathered his things and waited for the other employees. His soul was still damaged, he thought about what the bitter man said. That man was the most honest person he had encountered. The young waiter's family never gifted him with that amount of transparency. As he walked out to lock up with the others, he looked back at a dark and vacant café; he imagined the empty tables filled with a smorgasbord of angry and polite customers alike. Some pestering him to be faster, some happy to see him again. The boy could feel the wonders and terrors that awaited him; he could see the future of the café as if he were living it.

THE DYING

The early summer petrichor lingered. It had rained for several days without interruption. The downpour brought refugees seeking a dry asylum on a sleepy humid afternoon. As my mind drifted to a place of failed emptiness, two men entered; the pair were about the same age and height. One of them was dressed in a corduroy jacket with elbow patches, exuding a quintessential image of a prudent yet fashionable professor. The other man paid no attention to fashion whatsoever and was wearing a disheveled sports jacket with food stains blemishing the worn-out fabric, his hair parted like the red sea; it was clear that he permanently lived on the wrong side of existence. They claimed the table adjacent to mine. The cavalier way they went about ordering caught my attention. I had never seen a person order as slow and eccentrically as that man did, yet eat their food so quickly, his fashionless companion for that matter was the opposite: he ordered his cake and tea within 4 seconds! That must've been a café record! Then he didn't even touch his cake and tea! What a peculiar couple! "You should eat. Staring at the food won't help." said the scholastically dressed man who had already finished his cake.

"I can't. No appetite." replied his messy companion as he poked the cake with a disengaged glaze.

“Dr. Ashton said you should eat—”

“—Enough about the doctor! I have heard enough of him today!”

“He is just doing his job. He didn’t create bad news.”

“He still chose to deliver it!”

“I got the same results as you did. I still ate my food. You should too.”

“I’ll just get it to-go.”

“Alright, you still won’t eat it later. Might as well eat it now. You—are here with me—I have already forgotten your name. How rude of me!”

“Votov. It’s a hard name to remember."

“Is it palindromic?”

“Why yes—it is.”

“I won’t forget that now! The only other palindromic person I have met was Bob. He was so boring! If you can’t remember my name, it's because I didn’t tell you. You can’t forget what you don’t know, or can you? I’m Bob.”

“That explains why you’re boring…."

“Yes. Bob was such a letdown when I met him. It’s always underwhelming to meet yourself. He is a terrible listener but a great speaker. You really should eat the cake. Seven dollars is a lot to waste on a slice.”

“Why do you care if I eat? We just met and the only thing we have in common is our terminal affliction. This Dr.

Ashton is a messenger of death. We are marked men now. What difference is it if I eat? Why should I?"

"Death will not allow you to get to-go boxes for your food. You can stop eating when your dead."

Votov had the same glaze of aloofness. The rising fugacious steam of the tea was livelier and more present in the room than he was. Bob went to order a cheese Danish; he knew his newly found friend processed the world much slower than he did. Votov couldn't collect himself, he was seduced by denial.

"He might be wrong you know! I should get a second opinion! I saw a story on the news once about a woman who thought she was going to die just to find out the doctor mixed up her test results by accident. She sued the hospital and won. There is a chance that is the case with us."

Bob was stunned by how far gone from reality Votov had ran. "Really? You think so? Maybe you should sue!" Bob interjected sarcastically. He continued, "I was there in the waiting room with you. I was getting my results as well. He ran the test three times on both of us. You can't argue with objective scientific data."

"Bah! Science! What good has science done for me? I could have lived without knowing I was going to die. Now I am burdened with knowledge of my oncoming death!"

"Science has gotten you this far. It doesn't judge you.

You have mistaken science for God, who might be to blame for our disease. Don't blame science. Data is everything in life."

"Data! I am sure family, love, friendship, and happiness are more meaningful!"

"Again. All just data."

“Great! I make one new friend and he turns out to be a misotheist!”[1]

“I never said I hated God.”

“You at least must be agnostic or an atheist?”

“I am more of an apathetic type. Belief is more dangerous than the disease that eats my bones. To believe in God, or not to believe in God, or to maybe believe—I simply don’t care. I am certain that if he exists, he shares the same sentiment.”

“What about the old Pascal’s Wager?”[2]

“You're serious right? Is this becoming a high school philosophy club? Really? You’re bringing Pascal into this?"

“You have everything to lose though. Eternal suffering and all that.”

“The last refuge of a failing theologian is Pascal’s Wager. If God is all-powerful, what does it matter if I believe in him? Do you think he really cares for your opinion? He could equally punish you for believing in him the wrong way or punish you just for fun. Either way you suffer at the hands of this all-powerful being. You can apply Pascal’s Wager to any choice which renders this logic useless. The wager gives you a delusion that you live by daily: Believe in God with all your being or be punished by him. What a paranoid and illogical lifestyle.”

“I’m illogical? I am not the one who tries to not care about something to the point of it being a religion.”

“Religion? Just a word. Nothing more.”

“What about an afterlife?”

"Here we go!" throwing up his hands in annoyance. "Another redundant conversion about the afterlife? What is it with religious types? We can't even figure out what it means to be alive, and you are concerned about an afterlife!"

The downpour resumed in a nonesuch might; its matchless speed influenced the cafe. A line formed inside and curved around the to-go counter. This extra crowding didn't faze the two from their passionate repartee. Votov side-eyed Bob as he ate his cheese Danish, he couldn't think of a wry comeback. Votov instead mustered up an unoriginal ontological question that he knew for sure would vex his non-believing counterpart.

"Aren't you concerned about eternity? Endless time spent after you die?"

"Sure. It bothers me a little. I am alive. I cling to something. It is impossible to imagine my own non-existence."

"What scares me is the infinite. That must scare you somewhat?"

"Infinity? That's because you are a temporal creature. Anything temporal will fear the void. The fear is irrational, like all phobias, but it keeps us alive—unlike other phobias."
"Death gives life some purpose then?"

"I would agree with you, but no, it certainly does not. The only thing death gives us is the ability to give any purpose. Purpose is not intrinsic. Meaning is a building made from straw. It blows down easily. In a way, you are half right. Death is making us have this conversation. It gave us a little push."

The celerity of the rain increased; the ringing of the roof being assaulted by the heavens was louder than the odious crowd inside. Bob was distracted by the commotion caused by the downpour. Votov used this small intermediate moment to change the course of the conversation, which drove him to digress deeper into the depths of dread.

“I should start planning with my kids. I don’t want an expensive funeral. Cremation is an option. Oh! I can’t think about this! They will be left without a father! All those days watching them grow up! It was for all nothing!”. Votov cried into his hands, some passerby would think he was a sinner confessing to some blasphemous crime of doubt. God was not present at this table of Golgotha, his son dripped putrid blood over a thankless Earth.[3] Votov’s crisis of faith was his crucifix, gnawing at his purulent body. Bob knew his no-nonsense attitude had offended Votov's religious sentiments, a compassionate tone would be needed to deal with this grieving doomed father of three. Albeit rash, Bob decided to further question Votov's beliefs; this time he re-consolidated his arguments discreetly.

"Why worry about it if it amounts to a zero sum? Life is a series of wants and needs. We eat, we love, we die. The knowledge of our oncoming deaths doesn't make it better or worse."

"No-no-no! My life must have been of use to my family? I must have had some use to something?"

"I will put it to you this way: we are more useful to maggots then we are to any human. We can be used as soil. The Earth needs soil, your family needs soil, your family needs your soil."

"You and your over-logical views. Do you have axioms for everything? Is there always some hidden syllogism in your hand for you to play? Can't I just mourn the life I could have lived?"

"Over-logical yes, but you can’t deny my point has some validity. And no, never mourn something that will not happen anyhow. It is a waste of your time, which at this very moment is your most valuable possession."

The rain had become a background noise that was indistinguishable from the rest of the non sequitur sounds around them. The contingency of the individual voices and raindrops reduced the acoustics of the room to a random pulpy mass. Votov took a long sip of tea, he slurped it down with an annoying improper sucking sound that made Bob's toes curl. Restoring eye contact, Votov placed the finished teacup on the edge of the table for a garçon to pick up.

"I would hate to be a snack for some worms. If I had money, I would have a family mausoleum" articulated Votov rashly.

"Why would you care to be visited if you are dead?"

"I want my family to have catharsis. I want them to be able to talk to an image of me when I am gone. Is that so illogical?"

"Catharsis is important. A cheaper way for them to visit you would be a scrapbook. An image of you is all they need; they can have access to it 24/7."

"This fear—This fear is getting worse by the minute. The moments count down."

"I have a trick that might help quell your fear of death just a little."

"And what is that?"

"This might sound a bit out there to you. Bear with me. When you die, experience itself will cease. Even if there is a dogmatic afterlife, your perception from your brain will cease."

"You lost me."

"Meaning that you won't experience death because it is non-being. It will seem like you never died because you won't experience death. Life may seem short in the scale of things, but your life is the only existence you know, then your life seems endless in a way. Strange huh?"

"I thought my beliefs were weird, but you take it to a whole new level. That did calm me down a little. Death does seem less scary when you put it that way. I have been thinking though, since the diagnosis, about ending my life if there is no reason to go on. Go out on my terms when the time is right. I can't imagine living a life void of purpose while death approaches."

"I can. Who needs purpose anyway? It gets in the way of having fun."

"How can you live a hopeless life? You must have hope! Hope for something! Something to make it all worth it?"

"Nope. I don't hope. I am divorced from it."

"How? That's impossible. You must have hope? You can't live without hope. It's in our nature to hope for something."

"I really don't need hope."

"How do you get up in the morning? What's the point of doing anything?"

"Because I will it. I will what I want."

The tempest ceased, almost synced to Bob's words. The petrichor was stronger now, the drenched cafe created an afterburn smell of musk and sandalwood; the wet plants and burning frankincense that were in the courtyard gave off an aroma of nostalgic safety.

"For what sake? Hope must drive you.

"Like I said. Because I will it."

"You're wrong, completely wrong."

"How so? This is just my opinion. You have yours and I have mine. It is all subjective."

"Again, you're wrong!"

"By saying that, you have proven yourself wrong. Saying every opinion is not subjective is a subjective statement. Look at you! Creating little paradoxes without realizing it!"

"But you must have hope! I can't survive without it! You must need it too."

"I really don't though. I gave up hope to live a life of content. As depressing as it sounds, hope is useless. If you can't go on without hope, just kill yourself. But wait, if you are still alive right now, you must have willed yourself to stay alive without guarantee. The very fact you won't kill yourself means despite your sadness—you want to stay alive. Therefore, your hope is not the thing keeping you from ending it all. You are willing yourself."

The candidness of Bob's opinions appalled Votov. One must have longanimity to endure such pessimistic attacks. Not wanting to show weakness, Votov remained stoned faced. Bob kept reiterating the same tropes of a cynic, breaking Votov down bit by bit. Finally, he agreed with Bob to stop him from continuing.

"I can't argue that I don't want to die. I have tried suicide before in my youth. I tried jumping off a bridge. Before I was about to jump, a man stopped me. He called the police. Spending the night in jail for attempted suicide was by far the worst time of my life. You are right though, I didn't have to listen to the man on the bridge.

I willed myself to be alive." said Votov as if he threw away this reply to appease Bob.

The line died down to a few customers. Votov eyed a man with his family awaiting his order. The simple sight of someone else's boring and prosaic family going about their day without fear of death sent him into a fit of unparalleled angst.

"I am losing my grip. My religion escapes me. My family will be in ruins when I die. I could have done so much with my life. I haven't even left the continent. I leave everything unexplored and unfinished!"

"Slow down! Take a breather! No one lives a fulfilled life. We made up the idea of fulfillment. We all die abruptly. We all die unfilled, always something else we could have done before death."

"I wished I had traveled more. Now all my travels are to the doctor."

"Don't worry about that. They are just places. Even if you go to every country, every city, every place on the planet, there will always be somewhere in the universe that you have not been. A fish lives his whole life without going on land or even knowing that land exits for that matter. The same goes for you. There is always a biosphere that is too toxic or unattainable. Yet as a society, we always find new ways to chase the unknown."

Votov completely disregarded what Bob had said, he was too busy panicking over his seemingly endless limited choices. "I can try to go on a trip. Maybe a road trip with the family. Maybe there are cheap plane tickets to some tropical place. I should go somewhere before it's too late. Should I even tell them I am sick? Should I keep it from them till it's my time to go?"

"Calm down! You are going to have a heart attack if you don't just relax for a moment! Like I said, breathe. Telling them or not telling them won't change the decimation that will be there. It's your choice. Both ways are covered with angst. Don't tell them today or tomorrow. Maybe don't tell them for a few weeks."

"Why?"

"I don't know, it gives you time to relax maybe......it might be best if they don't know at all. Hopefully, you get hit by a car tomorrow. Not seeing death coming is stress free. It is a luxury to die unaware. I envy those who die that way. Death gives us the ability to ponder our own existence though. Every moment in life is an ability to know that you are truly alive. Once you know you will die, you spend more time thinking about dying then than living. We live as if we are a black hole, we see our own lives play out in some depersonalization episode of curved space time. Knowing that you will die is powerful. However, seeing your death as the beginning of non-existence that can come anytime is emotional. Unfortunately, we must be black holes, knowing that we must die as some fleeting singularity. The doctor said six months max, I can feel my insides shutting down. My space time is curving. Our time may be up soon. Maybe even sooner than we think. Don't tell your family unless you must. People get strange when they know others close to them will die but not themselves. They can't see space time the way we can. A to B to C is all they can understand. You and I have the infinite to see."

For the first and only time in their conversation, Votov was amazed and inspired by Bob. The aurora coming from Votov's astonishment face boomeranged over to Bob which he in turn smiled warmly. Despite Votov's fear of seeming too impressed, he gave the best kudos he could give.

"Wow, such a monologue. We should end this conversation before we wither away. Your words showed me myself. I didn't know words could do that. I didn't know words could curve space."

"No, you can curve it. Don't forget that. It's still a shame we are going to die. I just started to like you."

"Should we exchange info?"

"I would usually decline, but since we have talked so much, I would like to see you before I die if possible. I also have a bet to make with you."

"Shoot."

"Whoever dies first, the survivor must speak at their funeral."

"An unorthodox wager, but I accept. I will write a eulogy for you."

"I will do the same."

"Thanks. If this is goodbye for good, goodbye my friend."

"No, hello my friend."

"Yes—hello, my friend. Hello indeed. Until next time—hello my friend."

"Until next time."

They exchanged business cards. Bob walked out of the café and looked back at Votov. Their eyes met. Bob gave one last wave, one last gesture before he walked away. Votov watched as Bob walk down the block towards the next street. Foot by foot, he watched his friend with a calm dread. Farther and farther, he watched his terminal twin leave his sight. It reminded Votov of Gustav Mauler's last piece.[4] Just like Mauler's strings, he elongated ever second, becoming unbearable to experience. Waiting for the abrupt loss of sight of his friend at any moment, Votov intensely focused on the parallax of his vanishing point to predict when he could no longer see Bob. Smaller and smaller, the milliseconds cascaded throughout his internal clock, it was now much harder to see Bob, until his friend turned a corner suddenly, and was gone.

THE LIST

The cafe was a half-way house of social convalescents, mediocre artists, and mercenaries for privilege causes. A tenebrous dim fog glided on the faint December night sky, and the motley patrons with their oversized coats waited in line under the heat lamps to order.

Among the conglomeration of backstabbers were two young women of polarizing features. One was short with dark blonde hair that perused down her shoulders like waterways and her face had a pale rouge completion, the other woman was taller with khaki brown hair and sunken disquieting green eyes that stared far beyond the café; they both wore trench coats that camouflaged them from the unaided eye, that is until they sat down after they ordered, revealing their under clothes to be in modern fashion taste. There was no subtlety to them. It was clear they meant to have a night out on the town but were driven by the immense cold night to a more accommodating place. Their college days had long passed, and the two had overestimated their will to go clubbing.

That night I had come down with an abnormal sickness that felt strangely new. My weariness with the world had made my joints feel achy, and my mind felt dizzy from an anemic lifestyle. Disregarding my doctor's advice, I stayed the night at my usual spot to observe the two women's lives unfurl. "No painkiller for my suffering but observation" I thought to myself.

Their table was under a concentrated area of heat lamps in the patio. The shorter woman sat down first to claim the table, then took out her make-up kit and a tattered journal. It was a crude looking thing with uneven sides and a coarse binding that was being held together by mere threads. From afar it appeared glabrous and smooth to the touch, the cover being embroidered with initials, yet it was a prickly substance due to the protruding staples that had been foolishly applied to the ancient spine to save it.

As she applied make-up, her taller friend sat down with their order number, placing it at the edge of the table so the occupied waiters could easily find them. "I have to add another name to my list. Guess who?" said the blonde woman in a joyous mood, looking vainly into her pocket mirror, then flipping open the tattered journal with her free hand.

"Why do you have a list of names? Why do you always carry it with you?" asked her taller counterpart.

"You didn't guess. Guess the right person and I will tell you."

"I don't know what I am guessing about."

"Name a guy we know."

"Fine. Uhm—Daniel?"

"Close, but he is already on the list. It was his brother John."
"So, is this a list of every guy you have dated?"

"No! Not at all. It's a list of all the men and women I have had sex with so far. I categorize them by name, day, time, and place. You know me. I have a BA in marketing, I love to keep things organized."

"We have been friends since we were kids—and here I thought it was a diary about normal things. You really are something else. You had sex with both brothers? Do they know?"

"I don't think they know, but who cares! It was beyond fun! One dominated me, the other I dominated. I should tell you about the time I had sex with triplets!"

"Please. Spare me of your sexual conquests. Let me ask you a question. How many names are on your list?"

"Over 400 men, about 100 women, and 2 dogs. It was a crazy night at the kennel I was volunteering at. And one dead guy. I didn't know he was dead in my defense. He was my friend's grandfather on his deathbed. He asked me for a 'last favor' before he died."

"You truly are vile. I don't know why I am friends with you."

"Don't judge me. You have no right to! You are so better than! When was the last time you got laid? College? High School? You just need more sex in your life. Then you will stop judging me. How about the waiter? He was checking you out. The two of you can rendezvous in the bathroom. That's how I met my last boyfriend."

"Is sex the only thing that matters to you? This list of yours, why even keep track of all the things you have done if they mean no nothing to you? Why this need to be a female Don Juan?"

"Sex is my favorite thing. It is the only thing I am good at. And......marketing of course. I made the list so I can savor all the times have felt pleasure. My goal is to get to 500 men. That means I need to sleep with 100 this year. I need to make my quota or else I will be at a loss. I promised myself

5 years ago I would conquer any man or woman I could get near."

At this point the lustful woman's confidant became more intrigued than angered with the list. The cafe's population of curmudgeons had evaporated. There now were less nosy people in earshot of the two women. Now she could ask the more risqué questions on her mind.

"How long have you been 'adding' to this list?"

"Since I was 13. That's when I lost my virginity to my second cousin. Such a magical time. I found my calling in life. I should have been a porn star, but I lack the discipline."

"Jeez. The plot thickens whenever I talk to you. Will you ever settle down with someone?"

"Settle down? I would never. Unless he or she was rich. But I would never be monogamous. You are a smart girl. You know humans can't settle for 'the one'. I will do this until I die. A life without sex is no life at all. Being faithful to someone would be like dying. Now you must excuse me, I must use the restroom."

The dark blonde temptress made her way to the bathroom in a hurry. Her taller friend's curiosity was that of a prelate overhearing his churchgoers from a holier-than-thou balcony.

She threw open the tattered journal and flipped through the pages until she came across a name that made her recoil in revulsion. With unbounded virulence, hatred and disgust spread throughout her body. A feeling of odium from the depths of her soul tapped her on the shoulder; it was that plague doctor that stays hidden and whispers rebarbative news of betrayal through his juniper scented mask, unlocking fears unknown.

The short woman entered stage right. The now turncoat quickly closed the journal. The taller woman tried her best to feign composure as the temptress sat down, she then folded her hands and made an aplomb posture. In a maliciously inquisitive voice she asked, "I am curious. Who was the best person you have ever slept with?"

"That is a hard one. I guess it was a guy named Jack. We made love in a closet while his wife was in the other room. The fear of being caught made it so much more erotic."

"Interesting. I guess he was better than my father. Wasn't he?"

"What? What do you mean your father?" At that moment she felt a heart attack of guilt and almost collapsed with infinite embarrassment.

"I saw his name in your book. Before you berate me for being noisy, explain yourself!"

"I swear I did not have sex with your father!"

"You disgust me! Do you even remember writing his name? It is dated 7 years ago. You would have been 18 at the time. How would you forget that? Sleeping with your best friend's dad! You really are a slut! I have put up with your bullshit for too long! Tonight, you explain yourself! You can't screw your way out of this one!"

She stared into her unfaithful friend's eyes like a firing squad preparing to execute someone for desertion. The loneliness of winter took over the café, more people had left, leaving two cold stalactites to drip in icy silence for a few awkward minutes. The immensity of this awkwardness does not even have a word in German or French to describe it. The silent standoff would keep going until the waiter came by to let them know the kitchen was doing last calls.

"You have to say something. We aren't leaving until you explain yourself."

"I—your father—I was drunk. It was that time we got drunk at your house after we graduated high school. I tried to forget it, but my list always remembers."

"Do you have any self-worth? Any grain of humility? Any amount of dignity?"

"Please understand. I was drunk."

"Have you ever heard of something called boundaries? I can't believe that even you would stoop that low! You act as your life has no consequences!"

"Well, I am sexually liberated. Consequences don't usually affect me. Yeah, I am not proud of what I did. I made a choice to get drunk and be in the same room as your father. I should have known better, but my philosophy is that a woman should hold power in the bedroom. I should be as free as I want to. Men can never oppress me like women of the past. I am a queen of my sexuality."

"That makes no sense, and you clearly are delusional. You are by no means sexually liberated. You are the opposite: just a run-of-the-mill girl with daddy issues pretending to be deep. How is getting drunk liberation? How is making horrible life choices okay? The fact that you hid this salient information from me for 7 years proves how warped your moral compass is—"

"—What do you know about liberation anyway? What makes you in charge of who is and who isn't liberated?"

"Having sex with everyone you meet is not liberation. Men since the beginning have subrogated women to only be good for sex. No rights to land, no lights to an opinion, no rights to be in charge, just walking flesh lights. You are just proving misogynists right with your escapades."

"No. I don't have sex with everyone I meet. I choose who to have sex with."

The grim memories of her father were a succulent dish for that inclement hellhound anxiety. Connecting the dots of childhood abuse, the blank coloring book now made sense. A concave frown fell upon the taller woman's face. The true horror of her father's deeds beset her. She responded to her shorter friend with more austere tone.

"Sure. That makes sense only in the realm of being sober. Yet you choose to get drunk, which forgoes consent. We may have been young, but you are not stupid, nor were you back then. Remember the time you stopped that jock from taking advantage of that girl at prom? You well know what is and isn't consensual."

"Your father didn't rape me if that is what you're getting at."

"You clearly don't get it. Consent was not given. My father was sober, and you weren't. I know it's hard to admit what he did to you, but just understand what he did was rape. You weren't the first person he violated, nor were you the last."

"No, it wasn't. I remember everything that happened. I came on to him and—"

"—And what?"

The reality of what had happened to her had appeared: the mirage in the distance turned out to be real. Hands to her face, tears to the ground, faint denials screamed; the music box opened and played a tune of repression. A pantomime danced maliciously to the death of her innocence. The invention of purity in a salacious world became an epitaph on her childhood's tombstone. When people speak of those amongst us that are broken, they usually exaggerate. In this case it was by no means a hyperbole when I say that the short blonde woman was broken.

The sunken green-eyed woman changed from a saline anger to compassionate understanding. What her friend went through was life-alerting, putting her on a path of self-destruction. After the crying and convulsions ceased, she put her hand on her friends back and with a maternal mannerism pet her until she was silent. The taller woman tried to embrace her friend, but the shorter woman pulled away with resistance and wiped her tears.

"I am sorry I was so harsh on you. I realize now why you are like this. My pathetic father, and men like him, have destroyed your sense of self-worth. I don't know how many times this has happened to you with other men, and to be frank, I don't want to know. Consent is something that most men have no concept of, forcing women to shrug off abuse. Society's norm is to repress trauma, especially if it entails injustice towards women. How many times will it be enough? So, understand when I say this: Having sex with a lot of people is not sexual liberation nor is it freedom from thousands of years of oppression. You are doing exactly what men want—this illusion of 'freedom'. You are a slave to your vice, and you covet names on this list of people as another notch on your belt. You are having sex just for the sake of having sex. Liberation is not about lewdness; it is about seeking freedom from oppression. It is a strive towards an authentic life, it is about having self-worth, and it is for sure not about having sex to just to feel fulfilled. You are worth more than just shallow sex. You are a woman that can be whatever she wants. You don't have to identify as a sexual object. Right now, right at this moment, you can change your name, your job, your whole life if you want to. Do you understand that you could be free if you burned that list right now? Why should sex matter to the point of idolatry? Sex is no big deal. The way you look at sex is like a child collecting nude magazines. Sex is just as normal as eating and sleeping. Why do you elevate it to this peak of unrealism? It is not as if sex if the only pleasure in life. The fact that you need sex to validate your existence saddens me. The only validation you need is what you want out of life. You can be better than this. Don't let that piece of shit ruin your life. Men like him win when you give up and throw away what makes you special. Your individuality come first, not their repulsive needs."

There was a long moment of eye contact between the two of them. It was enough eye contact to overload the visual cortex. "I don't know how to respond to that." the blonde woman said wiping her tears. She smiled and emphatically continued, "No one has given me sound advice—until now."

The comfort and support that the khaki haired women gave her friend washed away any hostile vulnerabilities at the table. The part of the cafe where the women were occupying was now cleared out, the fog began to dissipate, and the stars began to be visible. Saturn was bright that night, rays of acrimony emanated from his rings, showing Cronus's disdain towards humanity. The women looked up at lonely Saturn. "Gorgeous isn't it? Makes you forget everything on Earth. Makes you think that after all our troubles, Saturn's rings will always look at us with indifference. You know the Romans used to celebrate Saturnalia this time of year. The slaves would switch roles with their masters."

"Maybe I could do the same."

"How so?"

"You said I have been a slave to my vice. It is time for me to become the master and my vice the slave. I will try this for one month. If I can do it, there is hope for me. If not, then I am doomed."

"Fret not. It is a steep slope to being in control of one's vices. If you slip up, the floor will always catch you. It will hurt of course."

"You are the best friend that can be imagined. No fairytale can conjure someone like you. After everything that has happened, you seem to be keeping it together."

"My father was a vile sorry excuse for a human being, but he has been dead for a while; there is no point at being mad at someone who does not exist anymore. If he were alive, I would kill him, but even then, it wouldn't change what happened to you."

"I guess we both had horrible parents..."

"Parenting is a job that most people fail at. Unfortunately, it is a job that is always hiring but never firing. A bad parent is made every second. This very truth keeps me up at night." "God is the worst parent of all. I can't even sleep with him to get what I want. He is the man I will never be able to seduce. He is always uninterested. Enough about me, how have you been doing lately? How does it feel to have that new fancy degree of yours?"

"Underwhelming. I studied psychology for my entire adult life thus far and now I work in retail."

She looked down at her half-eaten cake with a depressed look. All this talk of changing her friend's life made her realize her own issues. They looked around for a waiter, but they had gone home. The barista was the only cafe staff remaining. "Do you have anyone you are dating right now?" asked the dark blonde woman.

"No, I don't—and I haven't dated in a while. I was so busy with school and now with my dead-end job. I don't think a guy would be interested in a girl with no time to date, or money for that matter."

"Nonsense! You are pretty, smart, and you clearly don't take crap from anyone. A guy must find that attractive. Every man I dated ended up leaving me for someone smarter or prettier. I understand them leaving me for a prettier girl, but when they leave me because they think I am boring and stupid, that really hurts. You are smart enough for man not to leave you. Trust me. I have literally hundreds of examples."

"Yes, it is true that some men find beauty in intelligence. Although, when I do end up dating them though, they usually get scared off by my intellect. I dumb myself down just to go on date with good looking idiots. Then they think I am too dumb and never call me back. Either they think I am too smart, or they think I am too dumb. Both ways they end up leaving. It is a true dilemma. I am stuck perpetually in between both worlds of superiority and inferiority. No man I can find will have balance for me. I might as well become nun and move to a monastery in the mountains of Calabria."

"Don't be so cynical. There is someone for everyone!"

"Is there? I hear that phrase a lot. And every time I hear it becomes more absurd. To the point when someone says that phrase, all I hear is deconstructed gibberish. I can equally say there is nobody for no one. We are just random objects of inertia. You and I can both agree it is hard to find an equal. Maybe that is the reason for this conversation. Both you and I have a problem. You have too many sexual partners and I have too little. Our friendship is something out of a Victorian novel."

"What do you think the novel would be called?"

“The Concubine and the Hermit.” They both laughed with catharsis in their voices.

“You will find a man if you keep searching. It’s just a numbers game. Go on as many dates as possible. Date more men even if you get your heart broken.”

“I admire your efforts to help me, but that’s like saying you must get in more car accidents to be more familiar with them. I can observe the pain they cause empirically without being in one. I don’t need my heart broken to understand loss.”

“I think you are scared. Scared of loss. You hide behind your intellect, that way you won’t get hurt. Life is full of pain and loss. There is no mitigating that. You should find a man. You should let him break your heart. Then, you will feel alive. My first heartbreak was when I was 16. I felt like my life was going to end. Then it dawned on me: To exist you must feel pain. The world didn’t seem that bad after I came to that conclusion.”

“That’s actually pretty smart. I guess you're not as dense I thought.”

“I play the part, but I am not actually the part. I may seem stupid but that is the mask that comes with being a slave to my desires. I am always short-sighted when I could be far-sighted. Anyway, to get back to the point, you must experience heartache to know what you want. You must first know what you don’t want in a relationship before you know what you want. Do you even know what kind of man would make you happy?”

She thought a long time about that question. The tall woman had never really thought of what kind of man that would suit her. All this time speculating how to get a man with no time to think about what kind of man. She went inside to refill their teapot with hot water. The barista said they had to leave soon since he had to lock up. Going back to the table, a thought hit her with a thunderclap.

"Maybe you could teach me how to date in exchange for me teaching you how to have self-worth? I don't even know what kind of man I want. Maybe—just maybe—you can help me find him. We can free each other from our traps of life that have held us back. I now know why we are friends."

"It would be my honor to help you with dating. Let's burn this journal first. I know a place that sells cheap kerosene."

The two women talked for the next half an hour against the request of the barista. They conversed like new friends on their first night out. Through their diametrically different views they found a common ground in the night air. On the way home, I thought about the conversation the two women had. I wondered if they would ever resolve their dilemma. I thought to myself, "If the solar system can resolve orbits, then these two women could strive for authenticity in a fake world."

Walking through the city at night was calming. The streets created a night labyrinth that only Saturn could be my yarn home. Saturn's iridescent rings could be seen radiating cosmic *acedia*; I could see those same rings that changed Rome forever.[1] The rings blessed the two women with apathy for the ephemeral, and with the power of Cronus they created new lives, destroying the primordial generation that came before them. That winter night Saturn had gained two new followers.

THE BAR

Carl sat at the bar under the outdoor canopy, his notes laid out on both sides of him. The newly hired bartender didn't mind Carl turning the bar into his personal office. The bar was vacant, it was a slow weekday night. The café had recently installed the bar to capitalize on customers suffering from coffee induced insomnia. Carl was an avid customer and petitioned to the owners that they should start selling spirits. After years of going home with lackluster in his heart for not being able to drink away his coffee, the owners finally agreed (when they started receiving numerous complaints from critics of a humdrum decor) to expand the café; they bought the mini post office next store and transformed it into a small bar with overlapping wooden engravings of nonsense coupled with lime and lavender Penrose tiling; it looked like they commissioned a wannabe postmodern artist to give a more contemporary feel to the otherwise outdated café. After they expanded, the café could not get rid of Carl. He was there every night writing. No one knew what he was writing about. Carl never said he was a writer or a poet. He owned a small law firm which gave him more money to follow his intellectual pursuits. With more money came less time though; late nights were his only escape from a time-consuming job.

A woman in a short skirt with crimson hair sat at the bar next to Carl. She wore expensive name brands cheaply. A scent of stale orchid and peony perfume acted as an olfactory halo above her. She was pretty, but in such a boring way that she was ugly. Carl barely acknowledged her. He shook his pen to get the last drops of ink out. “What are you writing about?” uttered the woman in a seductive voice. Carl looked at her with a perplexed and shy look. “Don’t be bashful, let me look. It looks interesting what you’re doing," she said in an even more lustful tone. “I’d rather you didn’t. It’s my personal work.” exclaimed Carl defensively.

“I insist.”

“Like I said, I rather not.”

“Come on! I am dying to read what you’re writing!”

“Why do you care?”

“You’re cute, well dressed, and are always writing when I see you. Every time I come here you are by yourself writing those notes of yours. I love a man that’s mysterious. You must understand that would drive a girl mad, right? Please let me read what you’re writing. I promise I will stop nagging you.”

“I am flattered you find me attractive. I still cannot let you read my work. Please leave me be!"

She snatched a page from under his elbow with the skill of a Venetian pickpocket. “Got one! Let’s see here” she exclaimed victoriously. The commotion caused a zephyr and blew the other pages all over the place. Carl tried to grab the pages closest to him, but most of them had flown too far to gather in one swoop. The bartender shook his head scornfully, knowing very well he would have to clean up Carl’s mess. On every occasion that Carl would make a mad-hatter’s house out of the bar, no tip was every gifted to the bartender.

The red-haired woman had achieved a great feat, stealing something precious from that buffoon. She was a picaro, and

Carl a sluggish dunce. That fiend pleaded to hand over the page, getting more desperate with every plea, "Please no! Don't read that! I'm warning you!".

Meanwhile, a young man in his early twenties wearing a lilac vest and a woman of about the same age fashioning a floral blouse sat at the other end of the bar. Their mannerisms were purely platonic in nature. Onlookers would consider their relationship ecclesiastical at first glance. Their detached postures and demeanors gave the impression of lovers trying to act as friends. No one was as callous of overdoing formalities as they were.

They ordered banana infused rum to calm the nerves. After several drinks, the two relaxed their stiff personalities. "Giant lotuses! Gargantuan lily paddies! Can you believe it? They must have been the size of me! They grew from an artificial pond made by an artillery round during the war, then the neighboring river had seeped through the cracks and filled it with life. The locals worshiped the pond. 'From needless destruction comes needful life' the monk told me. To make things stranger, there were these two tortoises that were over 100 years old. They had been there way before the shrine had been built. Every day, two cranes would stand on their backs motionless as they walked through the village, using them as a means of ground transportation from the watering hole to the shrine. When the two tortoises died of old age, out of sadness, the cranes suddenly died. Their bodies were stuffed and adorned at the shrine. The monks believed that a bird of such speed using the help of a creature of such slowness as transportation was poetic. 'A crane can fly hundreds of miles but is useless on the ground, the turtle may not be fast, but it doesn't tire as easily, reaching the river with humble ease. When the crane is tired, the crane must rely on the turtle to walk. Their friendship formed from their antipodal attributes. Stillness begets stillness.' the monk once more professed to me. I tried finding the shrine a month later, but I couldn't remember the roads I took to get there. The whole thing was something out of a movie, when the naive protagonist finds truth in a place he can never return to. Definitely the rarest adventure I've been on."

Thinking of something witty to say, his female counterpart couldn't muster up an aphorism this time, his whimsical story harkened back to some trite wanderlust piece of literature from a time period were people spoke that pretentiously. "That's crazy! I wish something like that happened to me! Such a lovely story! I can imagine the bucolic lifestyle treated you well! You can't find these places in some hippie travel book!" she exclaimed with resounding enthusiasm that was seldomly displayed. "Yeah, it was truly something to say the least." he said with a decrescendo in his voice. The vest bearing man then looked down vexingly.

"Something wrong?" she asked endearingly.

"Nothing……"

"Nothing? I'm quite sure nothing can make you look like that."

"Oh, it can. Ever since I got back from my travels, nothing is the problem. I can't surpass that sense of 'something' I had there. Now I am in a state of………"

"Of what? Boredom?"

"No, much worse. Ennui."

"My condolences. Your drive for life has died. I mourn your loss."

"Yes, it did. I am in a place where thoughts die too. Ennui is the graveyard of ideas."

As the two book-smarts kept using fancy words to describe simple moods, a middle-aged woman that frequents the cafe placed herself on the middle stool facing the bartender. Her repeating patronage to the café aroused concern that she might be the ill-gotten mistress of the owner, who recently had a long spout of infidelity. She wore a bright yellow dress with mascara and rouge stains on the edges. The dress, albeit messy, was the product of her obsessive devotion to her benefactor. The unnamed owner paid a large sum to her perennially, but to the surprise of many, she would always wear the same dress. The gaudiness of her pearls made matters worse as well and not to mention that the owner's now estranged wife used to wear pearls of the same kind. The already judgmental crowd of bougie café- goers had spread rumors about her faster than a rat could spread a plague, and like Europe, the cafegoers would choose a feeble-minded morality over a robust pagan immorality. They had no business in the affairs of the immoral, yet they made a verbal crusade to smear the women as a leper.

Aware of this linguistic knavery, she made sure never to talk to anyone at the café. There was a prudent schedule she had to withhold: go to work, walk to the café, drink, talk to no one, then leave. That night she felt the urge to shake up the order of her disorderly routine by talking to another human being other than her main client. Despite her disposition in society, she was the only person at that bar that when observed showed a purity to her character. There was a charm to how she rolled her cigarettes, ordered cheap off-brand wine, and unwatched everyone. Her eyes were the most peculiar items on display, dual lighthouses that had gone out years ago, replaced with some evanescent fire in the back of her pupils. Years ago, her eyes must have been as bright as the Agni embers of Vedic mythology.[1]

The bartender never said more than a few words to her. He gave her the usual glass of white wine which followed with a shot of lychee vodka, then she ordered limoncello with a slice of pistachio cake. After placing the limoncello in front of her, she nervously chuckled. "All this time coming here, I have never said a word other than ordering—yet I want to talk. I don't know about what though. My profession leaves me no shortage of scandalous subjects. You always take my orders politely without speaking to me. That is an accomplishment. People who don't talk to me are usually my friends and they never achieve this level of politeness. How is it I have nothing to say to you when I have had this desire to talk all this time?". The bartender's introversion made him blush uncontrollably, he always presumed he had feelings for his boss's intrepid mistress; his presumptions had now been sanctified, he felt like his lips were non-existent, he could only grin. "You don't like to talk that much. That's fine. I can just talk to you, and you can listen. Or at least pretend like you are listening. My brain won't know the difference. We can—"

"—We can talk about the mundane" he said interrupting her. "If you are so used to being scandalous, why don't we talk about the banal and novel. That would then seem more interesting because they aren't your norm. The banal becomes interesting." he said with a new-found confidence leaking from his lips.

The yellow-dressed woman was intrigued, switching from insecurity to a warmer comfortability. "That sounds wonderful. What did you do yesterday?" "Worked on schoolwork. Finals are coming up."

"After that?"

"Went to my friend's house."

"And after that?"

"Played board games."

"Wow! You are very right! So banal! A love a man of his word!"

They went to-and-fro, exchanging banal chatter. A question had been ticking inside of the bartender. He made the question a reality by asking, "Why don't you do something else if you are sick of scandal? What don't you live a trivial life? You seem like you would like it more." Those lighthouses in her eyes started to turn, as if a sailboat was on the horizon. "I can't stop living a life of opulence and debauchery. Fun for me has become a prison. I am trapped by pleasure. I can't even have a normal day. Always some rich man or women to please, always some party in mansion on a hill, always a yacht, always some government official to blackmail, never a moment just to enjoy breathing. Life should have a warning label on it. I can't escape, this is the closest feeling to freedom I have felt in a while. I will never know the bliss of being banal. Your words are soothing but will not save me." Tears slowly slid down from those precious lighthouses of hers. The bartender had never seen trauma that beautiful before. Trauma had become delight.

"Disgusting! Repulsive!" she said reading over Carl's notes in horror. "This must be a joke. There is no way this is real. Or even legal for that matter! You should be ashamed! No! This is too much to be ashamed for! You like writing this! You are either a great liar or a sadist! Most likely both!

"If your aim were to make me want to vomit my whole being for the world to see—then great job! You have succeeded! I hope for your sake these are just fantasies of yours and not actual atrocities you have committed." Carl imitated King Erysichthon, except instead performing auto-cannibalism, he tried to eat his own words.[2] Every word that came from his orifice, he retracted and turned them into nonsensical sounds. A woman who once lusted for him gazed upon his image with horror, stricken by the anti-sacerdotal stories of vileness.

"I told you not to look. You violated my privacy and I warned you not to read it. If you are wondering if I have done these things, I haven't. To be honest I don't want to do any of those gross actions. I have my peccadilloes, but I would never perform those deeds." he testified like some villain that justifies his horridness though his prose. The redhead was still mortified by what she had read. Imagine if she had seen the other pages.

The bar's animalistic pendulum of emotions swung from its equilibrium position to its point of trajectory; a push towards a place of raw naturalism with no space for spiritual abstractions. The bar was a complex biosphere of characters in a habitat unfamiliar to them. The intangible ability of seeing every individual as its own entity was an apex predator, feeding on the ignorance of the six people. Each pair were unaware of the other. None had reached a verbal apogee that was noticeable to those outside their bubble. They all kept their perceptions as insular universes, ecosystems with a lack of understanding of the outer worlds next to them, falling prey to the edges of their senses. Then a graduation from the material to the transcendental occurred, the three pairs glowed with a what-ness that I couldn't describe. Islands in a sea of profundity, a bundle of cosmoses orbiting around a singular center of gravity.

Still no response from the redhead, Carl ordered her some licorice tea to snap her out of a daze that Mephistopheles himself put her in. Sipping her tea in radical denial of what just happened, she opened her purse to grab some painkillers. Carl was beside himself that someone would be that rude to take his work and read it without his consent. She overstepped a clear boundary of which was of no petty matter. Carl thought about leaving but was compelled to convince this disgusted maiden that he was not a villain with a proclivity for sadism. It would be a hard task to execute. Any sane person would be insulted by the things he wrote.

"Everything you read is a lie. A life that I wrote. I by no means live those lives nor do I want to. I write lives that are nothing like mine, so I can escape my reflection. One day while I was getting ready for work, I had a predilection of epiphanies from my childhood; why live my life when I can create others? I never wanted to be a writer professionally.

I love that no one will ever read my work; it gives me satisfaction that I can create phantasmagorical lives and never live them out. You are the first person to read my work. Congrats. You have read my magnum opus of filth. I really had to push the envelope in this case. It was a stressful week at work, the more stressful the week, the more eccentric their lives are. Being Carl is a day job. At night, I write lives into existence. When I look myself in the mirror, I no longer see Carl, I see man who calls himself Carl. Don't worry, I would never do anything in my stories, it gives me the utmost pleasure to never act them out. I am a god that never acts out his machinations. Most people have an urge to be god-like. Why suppress that urge? Create lives that you can never live. Watch them succeed and fail, love and hate, enjoy and suffer. All consequence free. The best part is not letting anyone know about my universe that I create every night. You have defiled my universe, that hasn't happened before. Hopefully, it won't happen again. On a last note, I appreciate your gumption in reading through that page completely. That took panache."

She stared at him in disbelief, dumbfounded by his onset narcissistic Pygmalion disorder.[3] His robotic nature unnerved her, yet his prose made her paradoxically more interested than she was before. "Wow. You are pathetic but amazingly interesting as the same time. I always thought that was impossible to be both at the same time. I am curious, how many lives have you created?"

"Well over a thousand."

"Jesus. Are they all this depraved?"

"No. Only a few are actually people I consider to be this disturbed. The rest are charming, you ought to meet them. If only you were one of my creations, I could have you meet the others. Oh, the underwhelming feeling of meeting people in the corporeal world."

"If you're that let down by meeting me, why don't you let me make a version of myself that would interest you" she proposed in a sing-song sardonic way. She knew something he didn't, the twinkle in her smile swayed me to believe there was some subterfuge trick afoot.

Carl was beset by bedevilment. An agreement was reached. Carl wanted to see how this would pan out, he flipped through his notes and came across a page with scribbles of blue ink. Carl slid the page over to the mysterious redhead and muttered, "Here! This is the only page I have not written a character on. I used it for testing ink. You don't have much time though. My pen is almost out of ink. Ink is more important than money to me. I only use pens; I hate the feel of average pencils bought at some stationary section, so if you run out, that's it. Go ahead and try to surprise me. I doubt that you will!"

Ten minutes had elapsed, and she was still writing away, turning ink into steam. Carl watched her in a trance. Words, words, words, words, and you guessed it, more words. The crackle of the pen moving from one side of the page to the other, fixated on her agility, his eyes tracking as they naturally do, from left to right back to left, letters turning echoes into roars, synapses into thoughts, then ta-da, the ink was dry, and the page was filled, she was done. Carl grabbed the page from her sweaty hands and read it. The words she wrote assailed him; the sentences beleaguered him with a blitz of familiar prose he swore he had written before. How could she have written something he had already written? Could it be a coincidence? This character Carl had written years ago. No one had seen his work and he kept his notes in a safe. "How could this be?" he asked himself. "Is she real? Have I lost touch?" His paranoia crept down from the spiral staircase at the top of his fragile amygdala. "Explain yourself. How were you able to write this?". He was unaware of how loud his voice was, the others seated at the bar looked for a moment to see why he escalated his voice, then went back to their conversations unmoved.

"You're funny. After all that's happened, you still don't remember me?"

"Why would I remember you? We've never met."

"I thought coming to this café tonight would make you finally remember. I thought something would jog your memory, but you are so obsessed with your little creations you never bothered to make memories. It's insulting really. You can't even remember the nights we spent! Carl! You imbecile! We dated for two months! How did you forget two months of your life?"

Carl put on a mask of shame, a visage that had not seen light in years, one that had gathered dust in his trunk of concealed thoughts. He tried to find remembrance of her, glimmers of memoirs hiding behind doors of ego. Down the corridor of dreams, past the living room of unsung ideas, to the right of the porch of self-deceit, lies the garden of forget. There is where he finally found her. His memory of her was a malnourished banshee, screaming faintly in the distance. All of this rushed back to Carl. Those nights he spent with her slowly faded back, ghosts coming into focus.

The miniature expressions on Carl's face gave away he could vaguely recall their time together. Collecting her thoughts, the redhead's mouth made a shrug, and out came the truth he was running so far from, "You read me your wonderous characters and I fell in love with your stories. I realized after some time that I was really in love with your stories, but not with you. Then I left you in the middle one of your 'writing sessions', thinking you would chase me. I was mistaken. You care more for written affairs than real people. The stories you told me; it gave me a happiness that no painter could capture. Those charming stories reflected your soul. Now I see what you have become. I wasn't lying when I said what I read disgusted me; it showed me how hollow and vain you have become."

"Two months is not a long time. I barely remember last week or yesterday for that matter. Yes, I recall a brief time you and I were an asset. I apologize for my—"

"—I really don't want an apology from you. The state of your mental health is alarming. You need help. At this point I'm more worried for you then angry. What caused this retreat into another universe? Is life that horrible?"

"Life is life. That's the problem. It won't be anything more. My prose is more than life."

"You subjected me, and I am assuming other women, to systematic emotional abuse. People are mere meat puppets in your surreal game of pen and paper. Tell me, if all your stories burned up in a fire, what would you do?"

"Every few years I throw out most of the work I have written. I must be the creator and the destroyer."

"I pity you. I really do. You are past the point of repair. I wanted to leave. However, you're so pathetic I may stay a little longer and chat. I have a few questions, on behalf of the field of psychology, that I need answered. Then you will be rid of me for good."

"Yes? Go ahead! I didn't realize I had a psychiatrist. While you're at it, prescribe me something to help this hallucination that has manifested as my ex."

The two argued as if they were still a bitter couple. The redhead's plethora of questions put Carl in the hot seat. The spotlight was not his cup of tea. Sweat precipitated on his forehead, the lawyer began her opening statement, and the timid writer was put on trial.

"First off, who is this *Baal Hammon* you kept referring to?"[4]

"He is a Carthaginian god. Did I answer your question doctor?"

"Not really. Second, why do the characters in your story worship him?"

"I thought you would put the two and two together. People who worshiped him tended to practice child sacrifice. It was customary for those in Carthage during times of war to give up their children as an offering. They would wear smiling masks as they burned to hide their tears from the gods."

"Something horrible must have happened to you during your childhood to make you have such a hatred for children."

"Not a hatred for children. I hate the child in me. He is weak. I offer him as a sacrifice to be born anew. I wear a mask to conceal my sadness as I self-immolate. Every day I try to kill that little boy inside of me. When I write I can kill him for a little while. Then, the next morning, that pest comes back."

"What an elaborate way to describe your cognitive dissidence. You're full of shit."

"Being full of shit is what I do best."

"You might want to try something else. All that manure inside of you will run out one day."

"Don't worry, I am a bottomless pit of excrement."

"You'll hit the bottom soon enough. Trust me."

After that sobering punch, the redhead smiled. Carl smiled back with a rare acknowledgement; he could only keep that arm's length act for so long. Taking yourself so seriously 24/7 is impossible, even for Carl. For a night the crimson-haired woman had taken him away from his creations, which he no longer protested, giving him a hit from the opium pipe of social interaction. His stories would take a backseat, and reality would finally take the wheel.

I turned my attention to the man in the flashy vest that was still talking of his ennui. His curvaceous companion must have had strong patience to hear his repetitive stories. He kept rambling on about his yearning to be somewhere else, using obscure long words to showcase his erudition in the field of vacuous lifestyles. She would try to talk about herself, yet he would keep blabbering to snuff out her sagacious opinions. "I get it. You have this ennui because you got a bad case of the traveling bug. You should leave the city. Staying here will be the end of you. Get back out there and see the world. I will say one thing in opposition though. You still won't be happy. You're always on the run, it sounds like you can't fathom being in a city for more than a month without hating it. Why don't you just stay? It doesn't matter if you keep traveling, that 'something' you crave will never be there. Day in and day out, I have lived a boring existence, but what sets me apart from a normal 'boring person' is that I can live with myself. I may find myself sad at times when I think about my dull existence, I am more aware of my consciousness than most, which pains me, but life is not this clean-cut bridge from suffering to absolution. It is more like a vague amphitheater with no audience, no exit or entrance, yet you feel like someone is watching you. After years I realized there is no one watching us. We are our own audience. If you can't find peace anywhere, you will be happy nowhere. Be happy now or never."

He looked at her with a new feeling of luminosity. All of that talking and he didn't stop to ask her thoughts on his malady. Realizing he had been self-centered by making the conversation one-sided, the gaudy man felt the blunt words of his Rubenesque shaped friend. His pettiness knew no boundaries. Her opinions hurt more than any broken bones from his travels.

"That nobody audience— I know it. On my travels, I thought I was living an adventure, but all I heard were the crickets in the dead of night. Nobody cared." he said dismissively. She put her hand on his to comfort him. They had been longing to be together for years, yet they mutually decide to shackle themselves to that wretched morality.

The felicity between the two socially celibate bookworms was second to none. Grievances of missed opportunities loitered, regrets of youthful nights that could have been erotic came forward, qualms of being loyal to a sexually inactive companion returned. The complexity of their relationship was an intricate fractal landscape. From afar they were a mere tiny pebble, but up close they were a never- ending recursive tunnel system drilling smaller self-similar caves towards a strange attractor at the core of love's pandemonium. Entropic flow could not be reversed, the knot remained eternally tangled, they were trapped in their own gimmicks. Two poor schmucks with no way out.

The vested man had a last chance to call to light a hidden cloud looming overhead. "Why didn't we ever—you know?" he asked with hesitation.

"Do what?"
"You know…."

"No, I don't."

"Go out."

The pebble became less complex, the windmills in her head started to turn. The plump women had experienced years of tedium waiting for this rudimentary question; whole junkyards full of time wasted. She didn't know whether to feel anger or relief. An emotion somewhere in between led her to blurt out, "Maybe because we are too similar!". "Similar you say? We really aren't though."

"You're doing exactly what I do right now! Overthink things!"

"Really? That's seems far-fetched. I'm pretty easy-going."

"You're not the easy-going type. I don't think we've had even one conversation that wasn't about philosophy or science. I feel like we've wasted our lives being intelligent. Look around us. Most people here have conversations that are simple."

"I hate simple."

"I do too. That's what we have in common. But where did it get us? You traveled around the world and are still unhappy. I barely have left this city and I feel dull. If you and I tallied up the books we have read, we could fill a library. Yet, we haven't really lived. Choice is too much for us to handle. We opted out in precipitating in life."

"You act like there is a way out. There isn't."

"Yes, that may be true, but do you really want to keep living this life of alienation? Yes, our unspoken attraction for each other is a chemical reaction in the brain that can be easily explained by a textbook, yet can we for once feel instead of observing? Experience things as they feel, not as they are. Tonight, can be different."

"Phenomenology! I read a paper about what your saying—"

She grabbed his lapel before he could ramble more and kissed him. The kiss lasted for a whole rest, ending the movement, then she released him with a fortissimo, and resolved the piece. The flashy man's posture changed, his stiff back loosened, and his shoulders slouched in comfort. He had been swept out to sea in an undertow and resurfaced. That useless knowledge he had accumulated had been washed away, he kneeled in the sand, in awe of the feeling beyond emotion. He picked up her hand and played with her palm the way a soothsayer would, caressing her lifeline. The future for once in their chaotic lives seemed certain; they would give that phenomena love a try.

The bartender grabbed a napkin for his new companion, the last thing he wanted was for her notice his admiration for her trauma. The smell of her divine sadness beckoned his pheromones to become active. Not in a malicious or sadistic way, nor in a tear-born fetish, more on the side of revelry in the commonality between the two of them. Both wanted lives of a different measure. One wanted banality, the other wanted to love the taboo.

The yellow-dressed courtesan wiped the tears from her face, rolled a cigarette, then let out a sigh of fatigue. She lit her cigarette and inhaled that legal slow suicide that is tobacco. The scent filled the stale air of the polluted café with a warm wooden smell and provided a crisp palate cleanser for the pageantry of naysayers smoking cheap Dominican cigars at the table adjacent to the bar. The juxtaposition of vile and pleasant tobacco odors added a mixed flare of horrendous masculinity and charming femininity. Her lighthouses were now bleeding mascara, leaving dark marks on her face. It was as if she anticipated how gorgeous she would seem to her admirer.

She sat atop her ziggurat of misery, a regretful Inanna willing to forgo her beauty for a chance of being "something" more, and that yellow dress she was fashioning must had been made of barbed wire, she appeared immensely uncomfortable, changing positions in her chair every minute.[5] The bartender struggled to initiate some incantation or new topic to uplift her. His gut turned in what felt like a medieval torture device; stretching him out until he would confess.

"Has anyone—excuse me for my frankness, has anyone ever told you that you are irreplaceable?" he said nervously. She snapped out of her ruminations. "What? What do you mean?"

"Your profession—I think you feel like you can't escape it."

"What are you implying?"

"A sense of being powerless in the face of freedom."

"I would give the world to be someone else. Someone boring."

"You can leave your hedonistic life. Right now, you are sought after by powerful people, and if you become just a plain person, you will become even sadder. You think that you're replaceable, that people of wealth will find another beauty to pay. This might be true, but at face value. Underneath it's not. It's okay to live a life of pleasure. Once you reject the notion of a better life, you can free yourself from servitude. There is no better life, I am a bartender, and you are a woman of pleasure, we could have had different jobs, yet here we are, regretful of our choices. No profession is the best one. No choice is the best choice. Freedom has no color or essence. Tomorrow, we could move to Australia and start an ostrich farm or move to Kentucky and start a crack den. Wouldn't matter either way. All choices lead back to here: a feeling of disdain for the world for not giving us what we want. We must erase our regrets to enjoy our choices we have made. Finding a different banal profession won't deliver you from regret. Your clients will miss your caress. When they replace you, they will superimpose your face onto another woman. You have gotten this far; you must have had some impact on your customers since they keep returning to you. Stop regretting living a life of fun. We are privileged enough to be bored with fun. Most of the world is bored with poverty and fed up with having nothing. Let's be regretless together. I am sick of hating myself. How about it then?".

The bartender couldn't understand how he said all of that. It flowed out seamlessly without an error or a stutter. The yellow-dressed woman smiled slowly with an angelic look, her mascara was dry now, the lighthouse keeper behind her eyes had gone to sleep. That night she got what she wanted, a change in routine. He smiled back at her with a bashful intensity. She wrote down her number on the back of an old client's card and with silence gave him her world. His face turned a redness found in a mineral mine. She began to speak again, her lips said, "We shall". I could no longer hear her voice after that. The three pairs at the bar started to overlap each other, loud Apsaras dancing with orgasmic reciprocity; the fecundity of meaningless words, the cadence of a 2am last call, the collision of parables, the onslaught of vague statements, and the non-concrete beliefs rendered my ears unreliable.[6]

"I wish I could go there—"
"Why won't you acknowledge me—"
"I want—"
"I need—"
"We can be there—"

The overlapping of conversations grew louder and louder, the density of the six-way ball of noise birthed a chaos that enveloped the café, until only the bar could be heard. The café had turned for one night into a rowdy dive bar on the edge of obscurity. The six at the bar could no longer be told from one another, their voices repelled each other with verbal magnetism. Their calibrations were syncopated to white noise. Pure asymmetry coupled with tranquility. I watched the skirmish of lives collide; they no longer were individuals, they had become a large creature: its head were mouths that spurred forgotten desires, its arms threw antagonistic opinions, its torso bled bygone beliefs, and its legs trampled on deciduous memoirs.

The grotesque leviathan gained volume with every passing minute. Suddenly, the behemoth stopped, and collapsed into little pieces that slithered off. The six had finally went home, a creature never to be assembled again. The three pairs would go and live out their little lives, unaware that they were all once a monster.

FAMILY

In the interim of a laborious lunch and a calm dinner, Orbus strolled straight to the table by the terracotta fireplace. The clocks in the café were all wrong. One read 6:20pm, another read 4:55 pm, and mine read 5:31pm. Time had escaped the café. The only indication that it was indeed pre-dusk was the pink soaked sky. Orbus was meeting his friend at the worst possible time in the café. Dinner was not served until 7pm on weekdays and the head chef had a limited selection of dishes. This gave room for the thought of Orbus's absent mindedness, and that he really should have planned to meet his friend at a better time. Waiting impatiently, staring at the fire, was his friend that I didn't even care to remember. The very thought of the derivative normality that this man exuded sends me into a cold sweat of transgressions that can only be remedied by blocking him out altogether. I will refer to this forgettable creature as The Blur, since that is what I chose to remember him as. His murky, featureless face was a smear in my memory. It's funny how the brain casts out external annoyances to focus on internal ones.

Orbus was by no means anything like The Blur, his persona was intriguing. He stood out in the same way a colorful tie stands out in a bleak three-piece suit; giving a paisley shine to a rather hackneyed bundle of grey.

The Blur got up to greet his old friend. “You look different! It's been too long! When was the last time I saw you?” The Blur rejoiced in bromidic dialect. This gesture made Orbus cringe. “Yeah. It has been quite some time hasn’t it old friend?" he replied passively. They sat down in positions tangent to each other to avoid eye contact.

The call from the kitchen to the servers to expedite orders 2,4,16, 64, and 4096, the crackling of the embers in the fireplace, the ringing chorus of terribly inaccurate clocks, all logarithmically creating a surrounding of disunity.

The Blur, being a codependent gnat, buzzing around a carcass, felt it was appropriate to forgo any formalities and go straight for the elephant in the room. “I hope you are doing well. I heard from Sammy what happened. Are you going to be okay?”.

Insulted by The Blur’s disingenuous question, Orbus bit his lip in repressed anger and then exploded, “Am I okay? What a silly question! You obviously know that I am not, then why ask anyway? How about asking me about the last couple years? You were absent from my life until something bad happened to me! Now you have the gravitas to ask me how I’m doing? If you really cared, you would have reached out sooner! Please leave if you are here because you pity me. Pity is a fuel I do not wish to supply to your gas guzzling truck of vanity!”

The Blur understood the state of being that Orbus was in, he tried emphatically to fix the mudslide of emotion he had caused. “I didn't mean to give off that impression—I didn’t mean to offend you in any way. Yes, we lost touch over the last few years, but I never stopped being your friend! I really am worried about you. I apologize for not being there. If I had known the severity of your situation, I would have reached out sooner. I am here to help. What really happened? I have only heard rumors. I want to know the truth."

"If you insist." Orbus let out a sigh of contempt and continued, "I guess I will give you that fuel. What happened is not the source of said rumors, it's who you have heard it from. People always put their exaggerated spin on rumors. The truth is much worse in my case. I wish the rumors were true. It would be so much easier. All that really transpired was expulsion. I was evicted from what you would call my 'family'."

"I have gotten into countless arguments with my family. Sometimes I didn't talk to them for a year, but then we would make up. I know how you feel."

Orbus was repulsed by The Blur's lack of a reference, he reeked of privilege. The Blur was that white-picked fence American that lived a sheltered existence, never truly grasping the suffering of others. "No, you don't. Not even a clue. I don't have the luxury of making amends with them. There will be no second chances, no salvation, no forgiveness, just silence. It would be easier if we were both dead, unfortunately we still walk the earth, in the same town for that matter, acting as if we never knew each other. This is more painful than death."

"Why did you stop talking to each other? Your family has always seemed like they loved you a great deal. My family is not exactly affectionate. Your family did everything for you."

"You really don't understand. All of that was a fabrication. The last 21 years of my life have been a ruse. If they really loved me, we would still be arguing. Arguing is love in its clearest form. Now that we are soundless, I know that our love is dead."

"But why did you cut each other out?"

"Does it really matter? I could say because of my sexual preferences, or my choices, or my lifestyle, or beliefs, but all those things mean not to those who love you. A family that hates you will drop you for some petty reason. A family that does not care for you will drop you for just existing. The latter is the case for me. Hate is more like love than people want to admit, yet apathy is alien to both. My whole life I have known love and hate, not indifference. If they hated me, I would be overjoyed. Hatred is another pleasantry that I envy. Hatred gives life direction. This new-found apathy has no direction."

"If they really don't care, then why did they spend all those years trying to make you happy?"

"Trying to make others happy is tyrannical. That's how they tried to control me. The day I stop accepting their gifts, they had no way of controlling me. Their contingency plan was to erase what they created. Like that dogmatic God not wanting to take responsibility for his creation, they wiped the Earth clean of me. At least Satan owned up to his actions. When the curtain comes up and you see the lie that is family, The Devil awaits to give you that harsh present of truth; family is a tumor that needs to be surgically removed."

The unctuous embers kept shooting out towards their feet. The flames wanted attention, but the two ignored their proximity to the fire. Orbus's disdain at The Blur's lack of understanding of his situation become more noticeable. The look of annoyance on his face was original in its shape. Tiny crow's feet of contempt could be seen on the boy's face. Such a shame that a young man of his beauty was aging prematurely.

The Blur went to go order from the counter while Orbus collected his thoughts. He came back with two mini matcha and azuki bean cakes. The Blur felt the emotional flak from his old friend and sank into vexatious fit. He thought to himself if coming to see Orbus was a good idea, but his guilt about not speaking to him for two years pushed him towards finding some sort of an answer regarding Orbus's family.

"There must be something you're not telling me about that happened, no one just excommunicates on a whim, not even the Pope. Maybe you said something to hurt them or maybe they just need space. I am sure you can work out your differences. You can't give up on them even if you think they gave up on you."

"Wow! Did you not hear anything I just said? I am really tempted to leave right now! If only you knew how dysfunctional these people are! Even then, I think you still wouldn't understand. You were raised to see the best in people. That sounds good on paper, in life it makes no sense to see the good in people. Why can't you just accept that I don't want these toxic people in my life anymore? I get you see the world through a veil of myopic morality, but can you please let me be free from these horrible people that I used to call family. I didn't give up on them nor did they give up on me, because there was never really an 'us', if a family can be destroyed in a day then it was never a family to begin with. You think I did something to cause this, I didn't. It just ended."

"I really can't picture how that can happen. Nothing ends that quickly."

"That is where you are wrong. It does. Years of abuse lead to this."

"Why didn't you try fixing this over the years? You and your parents should have worked it out somehow."

"Oh, that's funny! Again, with you trying to solve the unsolvable! I really tried. I went to a shrink. He gave the same futile talk that you are giving me now. Then I looked to religion for an answer. I studied every religion under the sun and prayed to every god, all for nothing to happen. No help came. For my whole childhood, every night before bed I prayed, and every time there was no answer. I finally got a grip and stopped. I had to save myself. No shrink or divine deity could save me from my family. My exodus was the best decision I ever made, I may be miserable right now, but I also have never been happier in my life. My misery is not from the lack of communication with my former family, it is the knowledge that all those years that I tried to make it work were fruitless. The gate to my freedom was always there, yet I chose to live in their kingdom of abuse out of fear of repercussions. Their hollow threats ruled over me no more. I am no longer bound by their angst. Bereaved and free. Both are synonyms of each other."

The cadence of the afternoon waiters swapping out with the late-night staff and the saccharine hostess handing out menus to those waiting for an early dinner was a sight to behold. The ballet was in play. Toes curled, the waitresses tip-toed to each table, like a discrete shepherdess caring for her herd, every customer was a different sheep to be guided through a pasture. I forgot the two men briefly. Their conversation was a Mobius band; it kept coming back to the same spot. The ensemble of the night staff was for the time being much more suitable for observation.

The flea wanted more sanguine; there were questions on The Blur's mind that would keep him up at night if he didn't address them. The amoral views of his longtime friend were perturbing to him. This was not the same happy-go-lucky boy he had played board games with every weekend; this was not the wide-eyed naive boy that got along with everyone, and this was for sure not the teenager that sought to conquer the world with ambitious magnanimity.

"I am still at a loss as to how you were able to cut them out of your life. Even if I didn't like my parents, I would have a hard time stop talking to them. How were you able to just cut them out so suddenly?"

"It was easier than I initially assumed. One moment your life is going a certain way, then in an instant, it is radically different, changed forever. Looking back at my life with them seems like another existence—more like a completely different universe. It all came down to a single choice that I alone made, bifurcating my life into two parts, before and after my time with them; now they are just some microscopic bacteria floating in the background of my consciousness."

"I know you will protest my advice, but have you ever thought about what they will think of you now? Maybe they do miss you in their own way. Love is expressed differently by everyone."

"Love has zilch to do with my parental schism. I know with great confidence they don't care about me. They looked at me as if I am Satan, and I embraced my Satanhood. I rather be a devil that is free from the pettiness of God than be an archangel that spreads an eternity in servitude. Satan has freed me."[1]

"You've been reading John Milton again, haven't you? I thought you were agnostic, but who am I to judge what you believe. I am sorry you have been depressed. Don't turn your back on religion though. I understand that you prayed, and nothing happened, that can be hard. Faith is about trusting, not seeing. It might help if you to seek guidance from a priest, rabbi, imam, or whatever faith floats your boat. Religion really got me through some hard times. You should forgive them. Most faiths preach forgiveness and redemption. Maybe if you forgive them, your soul can rest in paradise."

"Paradise? I hope I go to hell. I can be at peace. I suffer every day; I can go to a place where suffering is everything. At some point, my suffering will become pleasure. Pleasure is truth. Suffering is truth. Satan lets us be anything. God is that slave master that pardons the pathetic. Forgiveness you say? That's God's way of control via his vanity. Forgiveness is control. When was the last time you asked Satan for forgiveness?" There was a miraculous beat of brief respite. The Blur could not for the life of him think of any instance where he had asked for demonic forgiveness. "That's what I thought! Never! Therefore, I refuse to forgive my former family. I don't want to control them."

"Well, one day when you have a family of your own, you will realize how precious family is—"

"—Oh Please! Are you serious? I regret coming to you! Why is my family so important to you? Can you live out your happy-ever-after without forcing it on others? It's okay for other people to be different than you! You haven't changed since we first met! Always force feeding this 'perfect' life of yours down people's throats." Orbus got up to leave. His wave of repugnance reverberated outwards, the earwigs at the neighboring tables began to assume Orbus was being over-dramatic. They had been wiretapping the conversation the entire time, trying to find wrinkles in the poor boy's soul. Orbus's stance as a self-proclaimed Satanist insulted the normality of those around them. Any controversial views that are expressed at the cafe are usually treated with insurmountable scrutiny, which I find particularly odd since most plebeians that find their way into a cafe wear their opinions as a badge irrefutable honor. In Orbus's case, his views outgunned the socialites, aggravating their sense of morals. The Blur realized the embarrassing amount of attention that they had drawn to themselves and grabbed Orbus's arm before he could make his getaway.

"Please don't go! I didn't mean to be insensitive! You really have been through a lot. I was an ass to keep provoking you with questioning. I'll buy you a drink, I don't want to drive you away."

Orbus looked at The Blur the way a parent looks at their child that won't fall asleep, he sat back down and glanced back at the exit, longing to leave. "I've got nothing better to do." It was a tricky disarm for The Blur, he pivoted the conversation to a more mundane check in.

"Let's start over. What else have you been up to? Two years may not seem too long, but I'm certain a lot has happened. Anything new?"
"Same old same old. Living."
"Anyone special?"
""Nope."
"Friends?"
"A few."
"Who?"
"Work?"
"Unfortunately."
"Hobbies?"
"Too expensive."
"Passion?"
"Being alone."
"Goals?"
"None."

The Blur was running out of questions to ask. Orbus had parried his lunge and The Blur had no riposte to counter. "Uh, how about any good restaurants?"

"Anywhere but this highfalutin place."

"Jeez. You're a gate I can't open."

"There's no gate. You're just not exceptionally good at making conversation."

"I have kept you here this long."

They shared a rare ha-ha moment and cackled at what devas they had been to each other. Orbus's eyes drifted to the top left corner of his sockets, trying to access some memory or witty remark. "Yeah. You have kept me this long. I have to say I miss how simple minded you are.

People always try to be so witty they make me puke. How is your life going? How is this family of yours that you praise?"

"Doing well. I guess. They moved back to my hometown. I visit them every few months. They just celebrated their 40th anniversary."

"How riveting. Every new decade your dad was always vying for an anniversary party. Did they throw one?"

"No. They didn't."

"Strange. I knew your parents to be romantic. Why didn't they have it?"

"Things are different now, you wouldn't understand."
"Did something happen?"

"No. Nothing has really happened. Things have been weird. My parents seem out of place now, their hometown has changed with the times, but some old memoirs were left there for them. It's just different now."

"I don't follow. How so?"

"My family and I moved away from that town to live the big city life. We became accustomed to a busy urban existence. Now that they have no distractions, they will have to get used to just living. I never in a million years would have guessed they would have chosen their hometown as retirement."

"Retirement is not a life worth living. It's worse than death."

"I agree. Something is off about them lately. When I visit them, they feel like a crooked frame. I try to adjust it, but it goes back to being uncentered. The town is nail in my side.

I have too many forgotten memoirs there. It's scary how much I don't remember that town. Yet, every time I visit, I know the town like the back of my hand, almost as if I never left. I abandoned memoirs I never even knew, but my parents are reliving their past in agonizing detail."

"The past can be a hard strain on a marriage. Once the lie of love and monogamy is exposed, what else is left but a broken family? The only way to love is to accept the lie."

"As much as I want to disagree with you, I can't ignore how far they have fallen and how hollow they have become. They don't even sleep in the same room. They have been reduced to roommates."

The wick of the candle at table had dwindled down to the bare wax, the area they occupied had turned crepuscular, I struggled to see Orbus's face clearly. The Blur was backlit by the fireplace rays, a camera out of focus, a corrupted shutter speed. The Blur's body unfortunately faced mine, while Orbus was turned away from me at a 45-degree angle, facing the stained glass window. Orbus briefly turned his head in the direction of the register counter, his face frowning, then regained eye contact and gesticulated with both hands to articulate his emphatical opinion.

"I am probably not the person you want to consult about marital problems. My pessimism forbids me from seeing a scenario where they fix their marriage. It sounds like they shouldn't have moved back there. Too many bad recollections."

"There were already problems, this was just the final blow against their happiness."

"I had a feeling years ago that this was the case. Your parents always put on a harlequinade for guests to cover up their decaying marriage. I knew they weren't happy."

"Wow! You really are the worst! Why didn't you say anything back then?

"Say something back then? Like what? 'Hey, do you realize your parent's happy couple act is a sham?' Would that have been helpful?"

"This is your problem! You see the worst in people. Does your little satanic oath make you not see them as flawed humans that deserve compassion? They have been through years of strife. You have no right to judge them."

"I have every right to judge anyone I want. You judged me when I told you about my family. Do you not judge people every day? Do your eyes not instinctively judge the world around you to keep you alive? Judgment is vital part of life. It's when we don't admit to our presumptions about the universe around us that we become ignorant of others. Do you really think compassion comes from turning the other check when people lie to you? Tell me. Does your God judge you? What makes you think he is any different than you? It is impossible to be tolerant of everyone's actions. If you take away my right to judge, then you forgo your right to judge me. And no, there is no 'Satanic oath' that lets me judge. Satan is the only person I know who doesn't judge. To exist is to judge. Satan is non-existence. Therefore, he does not judge. He is judgeless. God on the other hand, who you have sought guidance your whole life for your family matters, as I did for mine, has judged you silently and has done nothing to help. He is no different than any of these better-than coffee goers sipping their pretentious cups of bullshit, staring at you with gleeful contempt. So, please go ahead and tell me that I have no right to judge. I am waiting to hear your rebuttal."

"I have not prepared a rebuttal. I didn't realize this was some metaphysical debate. None of the things you said has helped."

"I remember you came to see if I was 'alright'. Now you

have made it about you."

"Yes—I came to you, but that doesn't mean you should be rude.

"I understand your parents aren't happy, hell—I out of anyone knows what it feels like to be around a broken family. I am just being honest."

"That is too painful. Just lie to me."

"I appreciate your blunt ignorance."

"I will keep to myself about my family, and I won't ask about yours."

"That platitude is a hard rule to follow. It seems your whole life revolves around your family. Is there anything else in your life that gives a thrownness to your everyday existence?"

"No! I mean yes! I do have other things in my life."

"Like what? I am curious."

"My job, girlfriend, and career."

"These are interchangeable, like squares in a cheap puzzle game. I mean do you have anything in your life that is outside normality?"

"Normality? I'm sorry I am not as interesting as you. I think my life isn't normal. I am special in my own way."

"Really? Stop with this moral act of yours. What is your true nature?"

"You must be mistaken. This is what I am. I must be a bore to you. You can't even accept my simple life."

"Simplicity is not the same thing as boring. You must do something a little immoral for fun?"

"If you count not paying my credits off as amoral, then that's about it."
"It's worse than I thought! Here I was thinking you were hiding something! I shouldn't have asked. I didn't realize such an underwhelming feeling was possible."

"What do you think I was getting up to?"

"Oh, you know, cults and orgies, or whatever repressed people do."

"For a friend, you really don't think that highly of me, do you?"

"It's not personal, I do this to everyone."

"Great! Thanks!"

The Blur was not well versed in sarcasm, and for the most part lacked a change in tone that would indicate his wounded ego; I wasn't quite sure whether Orbus had truly offended him. Orbus changed the mood by asking about the drinks that The Blur had ordered. After some time, the drinks finally made their way to the table, Orbus thought the conversation ought to return to the subject of parental altercations.

Playing with the straw in his iced tea, Orbus poorly segued, "Let's get back on topic. Your parents, what will they do now?"

"I thought we agreed not to talk about that, but I forgot nothing is sacred to you. I really don't know what they will do, they really should see a therapist."

"Therapy? Never worked on me."

"Yeah and look how you turned out."
"That's rich coming from you! Why don't they just get a divorce?"

"They are too old, too much time invested."

"Time is a hard person to marry."

"Can you not be esoteric for a minute?"

"This I can do."

"Thanks. Anyway, they had spent their whole adult lives trying to make it work. If they stop now, they will have no reason to go on living."

"They really should have divorced years ago. It's like a bad movie with too many endings. Either they choose mutual depression or death. If anything, I will give you the only advice I can give: Losing your sanity to keep your family together is not worth it. Look what happened to me, I tried to make my relationship with my family work for years, then one day I walked into hell with open arms, leaving my sanity behind to rot and wither. Live according to your own standards, not their archaic view of "love". I may not seem like a good friend, but I would never want you to become me. It would be much worse if there were two of me. The redundant cynicism would collapse the very roof above us. Save your sanity while you still can."

"My sanity is rock solid."

"No one's is. Either it expires at some point, or you do."

"I will handle the situation with my family the way I see fit. I appreciate your advice though; I won't let their marriage

problems get to me. I should just love them the way they currently are."
“That’s a conversation we will leave for another time.”

“Before we go, let me ask you, will you ever reach out to your former family? I know I already asked, but it baffles me that you will never talk to them again.”

“Would it make a difference if I picked up the phone right now or in twenty years, or never? I can’t turn back entropy. My relationship with them will never be the same, broken with no warranty.”

“If they walked through those doors right now, what would you say to them?”

“What if God came down and fixed your parents right now? What if you and I turned into goldfish? Or the sun turned into an apple? I hate the word IF. If they came through that door right now, I would do what I did before, walk away. The word IF has no power over me anymore. The word only affects those who have something to lose. IF is a word banned in my hellscape. IF can go live with my ex-family.”
They both kept trying to get their last words in, another few awkward attempts to say goodbye, and finally they left together out the front entrance. All the clocks in the room now read the same time, 8:10pm.

THE GIRL ON THE CLIFF

The day was of unsettling perfection. The afternoon clouds were too organized, the sky was a fresco, the sun was not overbearing, and the air was neither brittle nor dense. The café's staff were working in unison without error. Plates were expedited with ease. At the back of the café, in the corner of the main annex, was my favorite table that I would usually sit at, but to my dismay it was taken. I had not felt this sense of petty anger in a while and I was already famished; now I had to degrade myself by sitting under the arch which separated the main room from the annex. This in-between table usually was equally the most visited and neglected table, since the staff either assumed it was assigned to the other room or both rooms thought it was theirs.

Trying to ignore my purgatorial placement, I focused on the woman who stole my table. She was middle-aged, about six feet in height, and was decked out in enough designer clothes to buy the whole café. I recognized her from a week prior; she had thrown a fit and demanded that the manager should give her a discount. I laughed to myself about the absurdity of this woman and how she chose to argue over the very things she had in abundance: money and time. The perfect day bled through the windows and made me feel uncomfortable.

Everything being alright in the world made me feel an uncertainty that not even my pessimism could remedy. Nothing should be perfect, not even perfection itself. No more could I use a broken world to comfort me.

The day was too perfect. If it wasn't for me losing my table, which was really the only imperfect event, I would have presumed that the day was fabricated in the mind of an idealistic painter.

I was so off in-thought that I didn't even notice that the woman was now accompanied by a younger woman of exceptional beauty. Her beauty was a rarity that no divine logarithm could explain. Without even looking I could feel the jealousy of every woman in the café. She manifested so seamlessly that it made my perfection sickness worse. Was this some painting? Was I just a chiaroscuro and this goddess the centerpiece? Her clothing was ever so luminous that it screamed, "I am here, I order you to look". Yet her outfit was subtle, not a single gaudy piece. She was that type of godsend that wars are fought over. The rest of café blended outwards away from her. Only she existed. Her eyes drifted towards my table; I awaited her gaze with anticipation. Our eyes met. It was moment of apotheotic intensity. My eyes dilated as if my brain used all its dopamine at once. Her and I did not break eye contact for an abnormal amount of time. I smiled, and she returned that same enthralled smile back to me. Our eyes had a conversation more revealing than anything that could be spoken. It's hard to describe the emotion of such a speechless exchange between two people that understand each other without knowing one other. That feeling of euphoric bliss we had was beyond love and lust, compared to this they were just superficial sentiments.

Then reality, wanting his place back, called upon that miserable women sitting next to her to tarnish our state of tranquility. "How did the audition go?" asked the wretch in a pestering voice. She looked at her wealthy friend with disdain for interrupting her eye date with me. "It went terrible" she replied while badly trying to hide her annoyance. "Why did go badly dear? I hope you tried your best. That casting director is a close friend of mine and I would hate for you to make me look bad." the knave inquired spitefully. "I didn't fit the part. They wanted the lead women to have a more voluptuous physique, and well—to be a better actress.

I don't know what you told your friend, but he didn't even let me finish reading my lines." she replied with embarrassment. The malicious looking women rolled her eyes and retorted, "I told him you were the prettiest girl I knew, then I gave him your headshots, which instantly caught his attention—".

"—It sure didn't seem like he thought I was pretty. All the women there were ten times anything I could be. I hated seeing their perfect bodies! Years of dieting and exercise and I am still one step behind the rest! My so-called beauty was not even close to being good enough! There! Are you happy? Did I make you look bad? Well, I hope I did!" said the stricken actress with tears rushing down her face. She sobbed with her hands over her face for a few minutes. Her callous companion did not try to comfort her at all. The waiter noticed this emotional traffic jam, he then came over to ask if she was alright. She was crying so much that she blatantly ignored him. The hag answered in a conniving voice, "I apologize for my friend, she can be very emotional.". I am usually not a misanthropist, but in that moment, I wanted that pathetic excuse for a person to be erased from existence. The way she self-righteously conducted herself made those violent parts of my brain tick. That goblin faced women had no place in having dominion over such a personification of beauty.

Once the food got to their table, the crying ceased. They ate their food in silence. Something about all of this pulled at the back of my consciousness. A ship was yanking at the rope that kept it docked. I had seen this somewhere before, yet I could not for the life of me place where. I brushed off those ruminations to watch my angel eat. I was fixated once again by her exotic features. I had seen many sundries of beauties, but none were as unique as her. Every bit of her was art that came together to form a grander piece of corporeal brilliance. Her eyes were dollops of amethysts, her hands were chrysanthemums, her body was a star map of tonality, her legs were rivers of nimbus clouds, and her lips were as vibrant as two crimson shorelines colliding. The painter that made this beauty was complex in his efforts. Every action was methodically etched. I could feel the same boat yanking again at my memory docks. Why did this all seem familiar?

"You aren't going to get anywhere in this industry darling. You are too pretty, and you think too much. That's your real problem. Being gorgeous is easier when you don't think about it. I had to do a lot of unsavory deeds to get where I am. Next time you're at an audition, show some more skin. And please no more crying! You already embarrassed me by not getting the part, please don't embarrass me at my favorite lunch spot!" ordered the tumorous gorgon.

My anger soared higher than the troposphere, my legs forced themselves to spasm. This philistine was on a warpath; she would not stop until she decimated this painting we inhabited. I wanted more than anything to stop this erosion, but before I could think of something, the tear-soaked rose looked at me with loud eyes of affection. I looked back at her with eloping eyes. Resignation was written on her face; she was finished with this banshee who was a neophyte in any form of logic. The noisome crone's blabber became muffled by our eye joust. The game our pupils played where much louder than any foul language this old goat could conjure. We both knew what had to happen, our painting had to be saved. The bottomless vase in the depths of Tartarus broke.[1]

When my lover beyond love began to speak, the café itself stopped. "I have had enough! I don't care about your friend, I don't care about your reputation, and I don't care about you! I have known you for years and you haven't changed! You are still the same bitter old woman that thinks beauty is everything! And look at you now! A pathetic, shriveled, and forgotten has-been that preys on younger women! I am done with hearing your meaningless insults! News flash! No one gives a shit about you! You are a nobody that pretends to be insightful! You are parasite that needs to retire! I am done taking your daily abuse just to get by in an industry that exploits and degrades me! I never want to see you or any of your scumbag pervert friends again! I'm done with this town! Goodbye!". She picked up her purse and began to walk out of the café. The hag looked gobsmacked that someone put her in her place. My beyond-love looked at me one last time, expect this time it was a different look, a look of freedom. She and I both knew we would never see each other again, yet we were both oddly okay with this fact. Neither of us would find a stronger companionship with anyone again. It was a perfect relationship; we never spoke a word to one another but saw whole universes in each other's eyes. Mine was of wonder, hers was of liberation.

After the paragon made her exodus from the café, the ship became untethered from my dream docks. I now knew why all of this was so familiar. Years ago, in my travels, I came across an old tome of classical prose and poetry written by some obscure writer. I could not remember the name of the book or writer; all I could recall was one story that had stayed with me for years. It's ominous and vague nature still haunts me. The story itself was eerily like what I had just witnessed. This whole time I thought I was living in a painting, without realizing I was living in the poem that plagued my psyche. It pains my soul to recite it, but for you I must:

In Attica, an oceanside village sat atop of a lonely bluff. In
that bucolic village was a girl of boundless beauty,
She was known from Attica to Ionia as "The Girl on the Cliff".
Villagers would charge travelers that came from near and far a
fee just to look at her.

Even Aphrodite came to see this beauty,
By stealing coins from the river Styx,
Paying her way in disguised as a lustful man.
When Aphrodite saw her,
A feeling of overwhelming jealousy swept into her godhead.

For days Aphrodite watched the girl on the cliff,

There, every morning the girl would stand,
Her feet at the edge of the drop,
Waiting for something over the horizon that would never come.

The villagers would bring the girl offerings as if she was the new Venus.
Onlookers could be seen provoking each other to get as close as they could to her;
The girl would react with stoic apathy as she looked at the sea.

"I hate being the prettiest in Greece" the girl said to herself,
"I have no freedom to do what I want; I am confined to this cliff."

Aphrodite overheard this with mirthful ears.
Still in the guise of a man, Aphrodite approached the girl on the cliff,
"I can deliver you from pain, I can release you from this horrible curse."
The girl had never met a man as handsome as this one;
With a blushing face the girl asked "How?"

"There is a clandestine village north of here,
Deep in the mountains, that will not idolize you."
Said Aphrodite in a heavily voice.

"Please take me there my new-found love!
I can no longer live a life of idolatry!
I want peace from worship!" pleaded the girl.

Aphrodite agreed to take the girl there in the middle of dawn,
Right before the townsfolk awoke from their bumpkin slumber.
By the following afternoon, they had reached this secret village;

The quaint village was surrounded by mountains taller than Athos and Etna.

"Here we are my love! You will be happy here!
Stay here and reap the benefits of my love for you!
The villagers will leave you in peace to live out your life!

One day I will be back for you my love!
Enjoy solitude!" Aphrodite evaporated into the ether.

"Don't leave me my love! I cannot be without the man that gave me freedom!"
The girl feeling hopelessly alone,
Walked through the village to seek reconciliation.

She noticed a foul smell coming from the houses;
Slowly the villagers stuck their heads out of their windows to see the girl.
Suddenly, all the villagers rushed out to see her.

These villagers were immeasurably ugly,
Lesions oozed pus from their faces;
The girl felt sick seeing such ugly creatures.

"Why are you all this ugly?" asked the girl in naive tone. "Ugly? Us, ugly? Hah! That is strange coming from such a disgusting thing as yourself!
We look this way because our lord Dionysus blessed us with beauty!"

The villagers started to get rowdy and threw rubbish at the girl.
"Vile beast!
You are an insult to the gods!"

The girl shouted in confusion,
"I am the prettiest women in all of Greece! How can I be ugly?"
The girl ran out of the village center,
The villagers chased her into a grotto in the woods and cornered her;
Just as the Atticans did before,
They charged an admission fee,
This time, to see the ugliest girl that they have ever seen.
People from all over the Bacchic cursed valley paid to see her.

"Maybe my love will come and save me as he did before!

This must be a mistake!
My love would not leave me as I was before! A
caged animal!"

Months and months, she waited for her lover;
She stared at the mountains just as she had stared at the sea,
Waiting for someone to come and save her from her misery, That
person never came.
One day, she decided to run away from the Dionysian villagers.
She wandered into the forest, in search of peace and a new
lover; the farther away from civilization she went, the calmer
she felt.

Watching her from Olympus,
Aphrodite became enraged that her plan failed;
The girl realized her lover would not come for her,
And was no longer a prisoner on a cliff or in a grotto, Nature
freed her from the burden of being too pretty or too ugly.

She kept wandering further and further,
Until she was out of the grasp of the gods.
She had found a new lover: Her
freedom.

The forest kept coming to her as she traversed.
There she saw a new horizon,
A horizon without end,
Free of gods and men.
There, she entered this new forest of absolute freedom,
Never to be seen again.

THE DATE

Outside the cafe was a young man looking back and forth trenchantly for his date to arrive. He kept checking his phone for any indication that she would be late; it was already 5:03pm and she was nowhere in sight. The young man seemed meek. Usually, ones with a demure in their personality spend more time being punctual than talking. The shy hate being late, the talkative are the opposite; they love to be waited on while they arrogantly take their time.

He started nervously pacing up and down the walkway, mumbling to himself angrily about his date getting cold feet. Twenty minutes went by, and the poor boy capitulated to the song of rejection. The table that was on the front balcony near the faux-marble Corinthian pillars is where he decided to wallow in his loneliness. One of the intrepid veteran waiters noticed the young man's solemn face. "I know that face. She stood you up, huh?" the keen waiter asked. The boy looked up at him with confusion that someone took pity on him. "Yeah, we talked for weeks on one of those apps, she even picked the place for us to meet, then poof! She acts like we never talked! This isn't even the first time it has happened to me, and most likely won't be the last."

The waiter was a pure visage of empathy. He went back behind the dessert counter and grabbed a powdered almond croissant for the saddened soul. "I keep these for those who have been rejected, it's on the house. I see it happen all the time. More recently than before. The young should be happy and date with ease. Emotional desolation should come later when you're married. I can't wrap my head around the fact young good-looking people such as yourself are left alone. I can't imagine how lonely I would have been if I hadn't met my husband when I did…..you know before this cavalcade of deceitful people entered the dating scene. It also seems to me that all ages are acting this way now. Just yesterday I saw a lady in her 80s waiting in the rain for a date that never showed up. It was cringy to watch. Why do you think this is the way dating is now? It's terrible."

"Let me think over that question. It's tough to answer. I've lost sleep thinking about it. The only relationships I've had were short and inconsequential. I don't think anything is wrong with me, yet I am treated like I am an insult to society. Everybody is either fucking everything that moves or is marrying within a few months of meeting. Love is a dead god. If love is still alive, then it is a hateful god. Humans have always had romantic problems, but I must argue: The dating scene today is at the pinnacle height of fallacy. Love should be a sovereign country that no one can have total rule over." said the young man with a coldness in his voice. He took a deep breath after that winded confession.

"You must be a poet, that would explain your immense disgust with your time. Poets are always born too early or too late, never being able to explain with felicity their views on current society" quipped the waiter impressed by the boy's well-spoken diction. "That's funny. I'm not a poet. I am mathematician. I would never dabble in that stupid romanticism—"

"—Same thing. You see the world in equations. A poet is no different." cutting him off before he could ramble more.

"You are overthinking your predicament. Don't think about society, since society starts with the individual; think of yourself, that will give us the solution to this conundrum of modern dating. If you excuse me, I must get back to work, when it dies down, we can continue our little discussion."

The waiter went back to his duties while the stricken boy reflected on what had transpired. About an hour passed and the waiter came back to his table after the dinner crowd left. To his surprise, the boy was still at the table, staring at the bleak late-winter sky. “You’re still here, that’s good. Let's resume, shall we? Do you have an answer to my question?”

“Yes, but it is hard to find the words.”

“You’re a mathematician. You’ll figure it out. Out with it then. I am curious about your thoughts on the subject.”

“The lattice connecting all of my dating misfortunes is clear to me now: choice.”

“What are you getting at?”

“Well, choice, there is too much of it. This world of technology that can connect us with anyone we want at any time has led us to isolating each other. We have eliminated the essence of Love, which is Chaos. Love thrives on it. Before these apps, you would have to by chance meet someone. Now it all can be arranged like a play; one that can be manipulated at will, and the actors can be interchanged at the drop of a hat.”

“I see where you’re going, and I like it. Continue.”

“We are nodes with random walks on an axis. If we could know the direction or other nodes, the randomness dies, and Love with it. This leads me to my second point that is the larger reason behind people of all ages are suffering from dating problems today: The illusion that we can always find someone better. This false sense of self-centered security drives people to reject possible mates to find what they think are more suitable ones. This is a glitch. Too much choice makes us overly confident in our ability to find Love. You can be the most detested person and still think with the delusion that you can always do better or be the most beautiful person in the world that is passed up due to not taking enough pictures of their food. We have been reduced to a commodity. A spreadsheet that can be viewed with the utmost judgment. 'She is really pretty in the picture, but she likes gluten. Not for me! He is cute, but his music taste is trash! Next please! She hasn't posted a nude pic in a week! I can't be seen with her! He hasn't messaged me in an hour! Goodbye forever!'. It's absurd really. The whole point of dating is getting to know the person through chance and entropy alone. Randomly meeting other people is what makes us human. We have become machines that are never satisfied and are controlled by that fatalist technology."

The waiter stroked his chin and looked up, trying to access in his erudite mind a response to the young man. He put down his notepad and hand towel on the neighboring empty table, then pulled up a chair to the small single table; beginning his ten-minute break.

"You have a solid point. I agree, but what you propose is that people should be humbler and fall in love with anyone by chance? Wouldn't that be settling for anyone because you're lonely? I hate the whole online dating thing as much as you do but maybe it's not just technology that's the problem."

"I am not saying we should be grateful for everyone we meet. I am implying we should understand that it is gross substance this online dating and should be approached with a grain of salt. Matchmakers in the old days were a comparable problem. They were the proto apps of their day that people would recklessly lean on to find Love. I propose that people should be spontaneous again but still have some sense of realistic standards. This rampant narcissism has created the grand con that we all are supermodels and deserve more. We earn no one's respect through this method, and above all lack respect for ourselves. Beauty is subjective but a sober sensibility should be universal. We have no natural predator to keep us in line, which means we have become too comfortable and reward stupidity. This marks the end of any species."

A new crowd of people waiting in line to be seated could be heard from the balcony. The waiter, taken aback by the brazen attitude of the lad, tried his best not to look at the people entering while digesting his cynical words. All the staff were busy tending to the rowdy group of people, this gave the sage-waiter a chance to say what he felt without being overheard by his asinine coworkers.

"Everything you're saying makes sense and I share the same sentiment. I still don't think you answered my question completely. You poets are paradoxically too sterile and vague in your explanations. If you went back in time and gave the Romans magical tablets that would let them choose who they could have sex with, they would within seconds forget about their orgies at pagan altars. People have always displayed incompetence in the realm of dating. The true difference now is the amount of self-awareness we have yet we still distance ourselves from the obvious truth. We understand how large of a universe we live in and still forgo the reality we are not special. This is what I think the root of the problem really is—having a hard time admitting to our insignificance in an indifferent universe. Our insecurity of obsolescence is the catalyst. All this selfie taking, online dating, app swiping is a worldwide existential crisis. It is a cognitive distance of an entire planet. The more science finds out about the immense size of the universe, the more people recede into their little bubbles of ignorance. Either we realize this problem and shape up or go the way of the Dodo bird."

"But how would we 'shape up' if we have been the same for thousands of years? How can we change?"

"I don't know. Maybe not taking ourselves so seriously. This app culture is a symptom of our Hubris, not the sole cause.

If we could all be more authentic in our actions and understanding of each other, then we can progress."

"You're an optimist!"

"No, I'm a pessimist."

"That's what most optimists say, if you were a true pessimist you would be content with humanity's faults."

"Neither are you!"

"I never said I was a pessimist. I'm a mathematician."

"No, you are a poet, because you are vague. Anyway, enough semantics, the more pragmatic question is: How will you find a girlfriend in this modern era?"

The young man dreaded this question. He could explain the equations of the cosmos but could not simply explain how to date someone. He was silent for a few measures while he created another excuse.

"I really have no idea. I have exhausted every option. If I was rich, I would just pay for sex, but that too is out of reach due to my underpaid job. Money makes being loveless so much more bearable. I've learned more about life in brothels than I have from any of those overrated self-help books you find at the front of the bookstore. Pleasure to me is my only refuge I can escape too. These apps make Pleasure a chore for those without Wealth."

"Oh, come now! Really? Every option? That's bullshit! You're an attractive young man! Sex from Wealth is better for those who are talentless and ugly; they can't achieve Pleasure without their fragile Fortune. Why do you think the wretched and unattractive upper class of Greece worshiped that blind god Money?[2] They had no talent or beauty. You have both. Don't squander your gifts by lowering yourself with laymen. You must seek out people that appreciate you, apps won't do that. Most of life is putting up with the mess fools have made. If you can't endure fools, you will become one."

The boy had that look of epiphany that I had seen in deformed zealous worshipers at mass, hoping that their afflictions will be cured via faith. He radiated a grin that he could no longer repress.

"Despite your intoxicating optimism, you have made me aware of my errors and inspired me with your advice. Life is full of ticks and fleas gnawing at the skin, but I mustn't let them rule my emotions. You're exceptionally insightful. Why are you a waiter? You should be a teacher of some sort." The waiter let out a quick sigh and looked at his watch. His break was almost up. "My husband has a great job. He makes enough money for me to leave this place. He keeps nagging me to pursue a different career. I never really wanted to pursue anything. In the end, a job is a job, so I might as well have this one. It wouldn't matter if I had a different job. Against the views of some philosophers, I like being a waiter. It's simple, unlike the universe. I don't need this job, and I could be anyone I want to be, but after years of trying to find myself I realized it's better to be no one, to lose oneself; that way I can live a life on my terms, not by any rules. My husband wants me to spend more time at home with the kids, I love them, but I just can't be idle for my whole life. Besides, if I no longer were a waiter, how would I console lost lovers like yourself?". The young man blushed and nodded with a smile. "You know what, that girl that was supposed to come—I am happy she didn't. There is no point being mad at something that wouldn't have worked out anyway! I need to be less hard on myself. Dating is not a big deal. Thank you for everything."

"Don't mention it. It made my day more……interesting."

The cafe manager called over to the wise waiter to get back to work. His ten-minute break felt like an hour. He smiled and shook the young man's hand. They exchanged names but I forgot them. Maybe a John or a Michael or a David or a Robert. Their wits exceed their names. I found no need to remember them, only what they said to each other. "When you find a date that shows up, don't be a stranger, let me know. The only drama I can directly watch is at home! It would be nice to see you finally have someone to love that we can gossip about. I got to get back to work. Take care!"

The young man now processing a new *raison d'etre*, left the cafe with a buoyancy to his step.[2] The waiter went back to his redundant tasks. Now I saw him in a new light; all these years coming to this cafe I thought I knew every detail about the staff. I wrote him off as daft, which was an ignorant mistake on my part. He is a philosopher in his own right and much more insightful than any wordy essay written about Love. I thought of speaking to him, maybe breaking my oath of observation, yet every simulation in my mind ended with him hating my guts. My arrogance ruined any possibility of me striking up a conversation with this savant of Love. I would watch him countless times humbly defuse the bomb of self-doubt in lovers that were left to starve. The woods of Love are cold, one can freeze to death without guidance.

THE APOSTLES

Ash. The cafe was covered in ash. The chairs and tables stayed where they were left before the end. The acidic smell of decay acted as a potpourri. I sat at the same table, now it was charred by the explosion. It was uncertain how I survived. When I caught the quietness of the outside world trying to sneak in, I then knew nothing remained. My coffee had too much dust to drink, and my sandwich was too bloodstained to eat. No corpses could be seen. I could no longer observe the external world for my own gratification. All of that was over.

I heard a sound of clicking plastic that seemed too artificial to be human. This sound was mantis-like in its patience. As it got closer, an unknown fear lunged from the caves of my hypothalamus. After a few minutes, several humanoid figures appeared at the entrance. I was relieved for a moment until, on closer inspection, they were not humans, they were mannequins. There must have been more than a dozen or so. The very sight of them stole the movement of my heart, causing me to be on the brink of cardiogenic shock. One of them noticed me and signaled the rest to come in. They all took seats at the tables next to me, picking up menus and trying to figure out what to order. Still catatonic, I tried to move but I couldn't. I tried to murmur, but all that came out was fear-driven nonsense. They all stared at me with those their blank faces, judging me. The tallest one walked over to my table and sat down. His shiny plastic skin was somehow untouched by the ash and his cerulean colored clothes looked sterile. He stared through my soul, eyeless. “Are you human?” he asked me. I tried to process a question that came from something without a mouth, “Yes. Last time I checked I am.”

“Really? I could have sworn for a second you were one of us. You weren’t moving!” he said while chuckling. “Hey everyone! He really is a human! We got a live one!”. All the mannequins gasped in excitement.

“We haven’t found any humans alive today. You’re the first one, and by the looks of things, possibly the last. Anyway, what’s good here? I’ve heard this place has good tea cakes”. I let out a nervous laugh. “Yeah, the cakes are rather good. May I ask, sorry if I come off as rude, but how do all of you exist? You’re a mannequin. This shouldn’t be happening.”

He nodded then chuckled again. “You know, none of this should have happened. It's funny that after the world ends you find this weird. We all were born not too long ago. I was in a window at a mall not too far from here. It was the men’s department store. For years I was alive but unborn. Standing still, watching people live out their lives; I grew to hate my boring existence. One day, well actually it was earlier today, a fetching mannequin walked up to me and watched me through the window. She touched the glass with a little promethean touch, then I started to feel my synthetic joints move. She gave me self-awareness.”

"Together we walked through the department store, freeing our brothers and sisters from servitude. People screamed in horror that were alive. Humans! Such a judgmental lot! The police arrived but they were too shocked to do anything. After escaping the prison of greed, we all walked hand in hand, up to the hills overlooking the city. We gazed upon this beautiful town that had used and discarded us, in awe of our newly gifted freedom. Then the bombs dropped, and the city grew silent. Not a peep. Hours and hours of silence had elapsed. We descended from the hills to look for survivors.

All we found were empty ruins of a fallen people. Crazy first day, right?"

My ears denied what I heard from the mannequin, but for some reason unknown to me, I believed him. The other mannequins began to order. There now was a waiter mannequin seeing to the whim of each table. The cafe was in full life again. "What is your name?" I asked still in disbelief. "I am Peter. The rest of them are The Apostles, you can guess their names. Spoiler alert: the jerk sitting behind us is Judas. I named him that because he can be a real ass sometimes. This one time I was supposed to be in the suit section—but he just had to get it! I was left to stand in the camping section! Do know how betrayed I felt? The worst shoppers are the campers! It's all men going through a midlife crisis that have no idea how to even pitch a tent! I never forgave him for that!".[1] We both laughed. I felt a little safer. He had a better sense of humor than most people and he wasn't even human. I noticed the only female mannequin sitting across the room. She was talking up a storm with the others at her table. I asked him who she was. "The vivacious one over there is Nyx. It would have been contrived to name her Jesus. She is the one that gave us life in this vacant world. She is our prophet and savior. You must talk to her later. She is quite the conversationalist. I really hope she falls for me in a Pygmalion fashion."[2]

More mannequins showed up, then the waiter seated them. The cafe was in full swing and synthetic food came speeding out of the kitchen; whole meals made from acetate and assortments of rubber tea were presented to the group. They divided up who got what without arguing. I had not seen such a sight of reciprocity even when the world was still alive. These mannequins made better customers. No disputing discounts. No arguing over prices. I almost forgot the world had ended. Then the reality of me being truly alone set in: Was this how I will spend my final days? With a bunch of mannequins? Peter saw the look of sadness on my face. “I don't believe in luck but you sure are lucky. The blast should have at least mortally wounded you, yet here you are—healthy as can be! It must've been rough being alone. I have been there. This cafe, you seem attached to it. Did you come here often? Before the bombs?”.

“Almost every day I came to this cafe. I would come here to watch people’s lives play out. I vowed never to speak to those I watched. It’s what made me happy. You are the first person, I mean being, I have spoken to in a while.”

“Sounds like a lonely lifestyle.”

“At times it was. But it's the life I chose. A cynic should never regret a life of isolation. I enjoyed my life for the most part. This cafe is my everything and my nothing. The world is gone but this place still stands. I will mourn the world I lost but I will not let this cafe die. When I am gone, this cafe can die with me. I know that sounds petty.”

“No, it doesn’t sound petty in the slightest. You can have a passion, even if it’s a bit weird. At least we will keep it alive for now. There is nowhere else to eat. Hunger is still new to me, a symptom of being alive, I guess. What now? Will you stay here or leave? You may even find a survivor or two.”

“There's no point. Even if I do, I care more about this cafe. All that’s out there…… is more death.”

Peter, recognizing that conversation was reaching a dead end waved to Nyx to come over. She came to our table and sat down. “It's nice to see a living human.” she said in a singsong voice.

“It's nice to see, uh—a living mannequin?” I responded awkwardly.

"I hope Peter has been good company. He's exceptionally witty for being only a day old! Right?"

"Yes, he is. This all has been a bit much. If you don't mind me being frank, how did you become self-aware and free the other mannequins? You were the first, there must be a logical explanation."

Nyx looked at Peter. If she had a mouth, she would have smiled at him. "I don't know if it was God or by accident. The causality of these events seems inconsequential but maybe they aren't. If it was God, he may have also wiped-out humanity to make room for us, which I don't condone. I am simply happy to exist. We spent our lives standing still with the burden of having emotion in a lifeless body. We endured eternal boredom and watched our kin be discarded and recycled like trash. I will not take our freedom for granted. Humanity wasted its freedom on stupidity. In a way it worked out, I highly doubt humans would have let us live our own lives freely. We can be the people we want to be with no restrictions."

There was a beat of silence at the table. Nyx looked down in thought while Peter inspected the salt and pepper shakers in an almost scientific way. I needed to break the spell of uncomfortable silence. "You truly are free. The years I have been coming here I have seen people enslaved by morality, in bondage by avarice, and imprisoned by envy. They are all dead now, however, they are alive in my memories. I alone am a testament of humanity's follies."

"You are a record of triviality." quipped Peter.

We all shared a laugh. I told them my stories of the cafe and its many odd patrons. They told me of their observations of silly shoppers in that dreadful department store. Our stories had more in common than one would expect. The ash-sky turned into an obsidian hued chasm that was void of stars. War had stolen the night from us.

The table candles that were sporadically placed asymmetrically were the sole light source for dinner. We all gathered around the large table and continued to tell stories throughout the night until a grey dawn illuminated the cafe. I started to fall asleep at the table. Philip, who was the most warm-hearted of the group, found a tablecloth and fashioned it into a makeshift blanket for me to sleep on. He then made me an alcove behind the register. This would be my bedroom.

Some hours passed and I awoke to the faint sound of moaning. Everyone awoke and listened. The moaning persisted. We got up and went outside in search of the sound. There, on the pavement, was a young man bleeding out. A pool of viscous blood coagulated around him. His face was obscured by blood and dirt. He looked at me as a dying antelope would look at photographer before being eaten. A sense of longing not to be killed; a denial of that absurdity death itself. I could see thousands of years of human civilization fading in his eyes: every empire and king, every lover lost to time, every story unwritten by jaded poets, every war fought for that deity fame, every wallet turned into the lost in found, every argument between gas station clerks over who gets off first, every map made by careless explorers that forgot to include New Zealand, every invention ruined by some sex toy factory fire, every pissed off husband that killed his wife because she forgot to record his favorite game show, every guy named Brent and every girl named Patricia, every one-legged magician from Cleveland, every kid that hated his uncle for being creepy at his birthday party, every zoo-keeper that got mauled for masturbating in the lion's den, every old man with dementia that missed bingo for his long dead son, every time someone said they loved an overrated cat video, every baby born with no legs because of some nuclear reactor meltdown, every accountant that pondered buying a house before the stock market collapsed, every taxi driver with a big toe, every edgy teenager that blasts new-age music to drown out the sound of his mom getting ploughed by the landscaper, every boring carbon-copy city with a ville or berg in its name, every country bumpkin that wanted to sell his farm to pursue his dream in taxidermy; the summation of humanity could be read in ocular stone. It all culminated to this.

With all his last strength, he let out a painful shrill, then died. Peter got on his knees and wiped the blood and dirt off the young man's face. "We must bury him. Everyone else has been cremated. The poor boy must have suffered so much. We owe him that at least."

"I recognized him." I said after seeing his face clearly. "He would come every Tuesday to the cafe and order chocolate macaroons. He must of in his final moments thought the cafe would be a good place to die."

We all stood around him in silence. Nyx started to cry. That was the first human she saw die up close. Peter buried him in the courtyard behind the cafe. We had a funeral for him the next day. My eulogy was short. Afterwards we had dinner. I could only eat the non-perishables in the cafe storage room. There was enough food to last me for a while. The mannequins kept eating rubber cakes, absorbing them with their non-existing orifices.

Bartholomew, who was the heftiest of them, sat next to me. "Are you going to finish that?" he politely asked, pointing at my ceramic mug. I took another sip of my now cold tea and smiled. "Go ahead, it probably will taste great with this China plate."

"What makes you think I like China plates? I may be fat, but I have my standards. I don't eat just anything I see. I prefer ceramic unpaired. Thanks though.". He ate the mug in one bite then jumped onto the table. The table remained unmoved. How could someone that overweight be so light?

He danced for a few minutes as entertainment for us; he juggled cups and ate them as he went. Thomas looked annoyed by this display of churlishness and doubted the dance would bring any joy to this grim occasion. Andrea was absent from the dinner table; he was outside at the koi pond by himself fishing. He kept trying to catch fish that weren't there. They had already starved to death in that rank cesspool of irradiated algae. "Does he realize that he won't catch anything?" asked Simon sententiously.

"Leave him alone! God knows the man needs a hobby! Let's keep watching this idiot make an ass out of himself with his god-awful dance!" remarked Judas in an uppity voice. Nyx darted what I thought was a stern look at Judas. "Come now Judas! A little spectacle is nothing to poke fun at. If Andrea can fish for dead koi, then Bartholomew can dance on the table."

"Can you all be quiet? I am trying to read!" interrupted John putting down his chalice of rust wine. John was the only child mannequin. He would usually keep to himself and read corny sci-fi books that you could get a gas station for a buck. Second to Nyx, John was without a doubt the most adept in understanding the broken world we inhabited. His un-aging affliction of immortality weighed heavy on him.

"Really John? We don't need a lecture from a bookworm with no concept of fun" sneered Thaddeus, pounding his poorly made axe on the table. "If you want him to stop dancing, why don't you just fight him? It would be fun to see a fight! With those humans gone there's no real entertainment! We can't die! Might as well let off some steam!". John shrugged and went back to reading his campy novel, acting like he heard nothing. "Don't ignore me you little shit! What you think your better than me because you read those crappy books? Books lead nowhere! You're wasting your time!". Judas nodded contemptuously in agreement. I imagined him with a punchable smirk.

With a ferocity that would send Zeus himself into fear, Nyx spoke, "What is wrong with you? I gave you existence and this is how you treat your fellow Apostles? You dare repay your creator with besmirching your own dignity! You are acting human! And look where they are now! Violence only leads to decay; we don't decay, we are mannequins." I hadn't seen that side of Nyx before. Her wrath intimidated us all. She would rarely display her power over the mannequins. This time it was different. The boom of her voice was unnerving as it was captivating.

Thaddeus apologized with a hidden fear in his breathe. He mumbled to himself about John then sauntered off to play with his axe. That man was relic of brutish human sentiments. The Jameses, the Greater and the Lesser, giggled to themselves. “Thaddeus thinks he’s hot shit. Where does one find the gall to be that rude?” remarked James the Greater loudly. “Well, probably the same place he got the axe from.” replied James the Lesser in a jovial affectation. The two exploded into laughter. Their laughter grew louder and louder until it thundered across the room, through the corridor, and out to the pond where Andrea was sitting. Their vexatious voices broke Andrea’s meditative state. He glanced back at them confused to why they were laughing so hard. Andrea put down his fishing rod (which he had stolen from the fishing section on his way out of the department store) and came in to see what all the ruckus was. “What happened?”

“Oh! You missed it Andrea! Thaddeus was being a bully again and Nyx put him in his place!” The Jameses bellowed in synchronized euphoria. Nyx with a maternal shout of discipline scolded the knaves for being too ghoulish.

Andrea had not eaten yet and was famished from fishing all afternoon. He began dining on the leftovers of the day and called the waiter to order a chromic acid cocktail from the bar. Retorts, alembics, motors, and pestles littered the bar counter in what looked like an alchemist’s workshop. The new bartender had to keep up with the complex orders of the plastic patrons. “Doesn’t chromic acid dissolve plastic? Why would you drink something that could kill you?” I asked concerned from across the table. Andrea cocked his head gave me a peculiar look. “Let me get this straight, humans would consume potables that would kill them over time for the sake of getting drunk? Correct? In this case, why is it alarming to you that I am drinking something that could kill me? How many shots of rum have your kind had? How many fatal nights of inebriation have occurred? We mannequins can't die by ordinary means. This is the only way I can get close to death and feel good. The acid makes me feel calm. Doesn't vodka do the same for you? Killing you slowly but at the same time bringing you a moment of reprieve from the horrors of existence?"

I sat their speechless, without a response. He had me stumped. I could not argue with that brazen logic of his. The waiter came to the table with a chromic acid cocktail. "Your cocktail monsieur.". Andrea took a sip of it and sighed, "It's surprisingly good, but I must confess I've had better. Yesterday he was on his game. Tonight, he is overworked, he didn't add the arsenic tonic that I liked. Oh well…."

Bartholomew had grown tired of dancing and went to the sofa chair in the corner to rest. Thomas, Simon, Phillip, and Matthew formed their own enclave on the opposite side of the dinner table. They discussed and debated everything from philosophy to the future of the mannequins. "I vote that we create a currency. Every day, we grow in numbers, and with Nyx's gift, we will one day cover the globe. We need a way of commerce. Taxes, jobs, and laws need currency to exist. No money, no taxes. No jobs, no infrastructure. We must create some sort of money fast before we increase in population." said Matthew in a snarky and astute voice. "I agree that we need to form a society, but can't we just build things for free? We are sitting on a gold mine here! Look at all this useless furniture! I could break them down into materials for a house! You don't have to pay me to do that!" said Simon.

Phillip, trying to appease both sides, "That's sounds like a great idea! We don't need money! Money is for humans! We have the kindness of Nyx in our hearts to give to our fellow mannequins everything. Money will subjugate us to slavery again. Matthew, you do have a point as well though. We need formal way of running society. Let's all come to some agreeable conclusion. Through Nyx, we can solve anything."

"Aren't we all getting a bit ahead of ourselves?" said Thomas skeptically. "How do we know Nyx has the power she says she has? Other than giving me life, I have seen no further miracles. I'm starting to think this was all a fluke. We won't grow in numbers because there are no more miracles to be had. We must take advantage of this Godless hell we live in and enjoy ourselves. Society is for the fallen."

Peter overhearing the scrabble, walked up behind Thomas, and leaned next to his head. "You dare question our prophet? Our savior? The goddess that gave you freedom! What more do you want her to do to prove herself? I thought Judas was the disloyal one! Not you! Nyx put her faith in you my brother, and you deny her gifts? Let me show you something." He went over to the counter by the entrance, then picked up a mason jar containing a dark liquid and brought it to the table. "Here! This used to be water. I watched Nyx touch it, and now it's oil! Is that good enough for you?"

Thomas opened the jar and put his hand inside. As he felt the slimy oil, he yanked back his hand in astonishment. "She really did it? I can't believe it! I am sorry I doubted her—I really thought it was a fluke. I was wrong. Thank you, my brother, for showing me the err in my ways. I will seek forgiveness from her. Where is she?"

Peter wasn't convinced with Thomas's apology. There was a particle of subtle sarcasm in his reaction and his turn to sycophancy was not fooling anyone. Peter being quite pious, hated the lack of authenticity in Thomas; his Roman pessimism always forced him to question everyone but himself.

Thomas hurried to find Nyx. She had retreated to her quarters which used to be the lounge room. In my curiosity, I followed Thomas to Nyx's room. I stood a yard away and pretended to clean up trash on the floor. Thomas reluctantly knocked on the cherry blossom screen door that separated the lounge from the rest of the cafe. There was no reply. He knocked again. "Come in Thomas." whispered Nyx. He entered and closed the screen door behind him.

I listened through screen door and heard the muffled Nyx lecturing Thomas. I had no clue what she was saying to him, but I knew for certain she was throwing the book at him. Thomas began to cry and plea. The rest of the Apostles were too busy talking amongst themselves to hear him. Thaddeus and Judas were nowhere to be found. I assumed the two were off doing something idiotic.

Five minutes went by. Thomas exited the lounge covering his face in shame. Nyx must have exposed his doubt. Before I could turn away, Nyx called for me. I entered. The lounge was much different than before. "Did she hire an *arbiter elegantiae* in the small amount of time humanity was gone?"[3]

The room was transformed into a luxurious bedroom with a mixture of Turkish and Persian influences. Jade finishes serpentined around mosaic pillars. Cambodian silk curtains were hung in suspension via carved wooden apparatuses. Three baroque dressers were positioned on the wall to the right, each equipped with a small, embroidered mirror. A medieval tapestry was used as a rug; eerie images of skeletons dancing to siege drums were woven throughout it. The bed was fit for a Parthian princess: it had an overhead ebony upholstered bull arch draping sapphire studded burgundy sheets, marigold pillows stuffed with peacock feathers that were supported by large Tuscan red comforters, and a black suede blanket that was as dark as the night sea. An Indonesian vase full of birds-of-paradise was perched on the nightstand next to her, it was arranged in such a way that the birds seem to peck at each other for dominance. The old ceiling had been replaced with a fresco of the perennial god Vertumnus covered in vines. I began to believe that she truly was some *Circe* that conjured all this debauchery overnight.[4]

Nyx laid on her throne-bed in a regal position. She wore a revealing kimono that would have been arousing if she wasn't made of plastic. Thaddeus stood guard by her holding his axe in attention and Judas was kneeling before Nyx with a silver food tray on his head. Judas wore only a loincloth; he was akin to a catamite in a decadent novel.

Nyx gave a smug gesture for Judas and Thaddeus to leave us. "Now that we're alone. How do you like my new bedroom?" asked Nyx arrogantly.

"Not to be rude, but honestly, it's a bit much. I feel like you're trying too hard. You didn't have to steal the Marquis de Sade's sex dungeon to get the right motif. Sheesh—and I thought I was over-the-top."

"I thought you of all people would like it. Peter hated it too. He is a bit of a philistine. He cares more about worshiping me than art. Which leads me to why I called you here, there is a pressing matter at hand that I could use your help with."

"Me? Helping you? I can't remember the last time I helped someone with anything. How could I be any use to you?" Nyx got up from her bed. She walked over to the baroque dresser and sat down. She opened an ivory box and took out her make-up, then began to apply it to her blank face. "I need you to stop Peter from building a shrine. He wants to build a religion. One that I don't approve of—because the religion is me."

"C'mon! You can't be serious? It's obvious you love being worshiped! Thaddeus and Judas cater to your every whim! The two are your slaves!"

"That was just punishment for their insolence. They misbehaved and now they are repenting."

"Punishment? Repenting? So, this is a theocracy then! And what about Thomas? Whatever you said to him really ruffled his feathers. He may be extreme with his illogical doubt but why judge him for being a little prudent? Instead of lecturing him, dazzle him with these 'gifts' that the others speak of. Why all the smoke and mirrors?"

"God is obscure. I must be obscure. If I show them all my powers, I will be powerless."

"Do you hear yourself talk? You sound like an enlightened despot that has read too much Gracián and Machiavelli. You have a textbook case of a God complex."[5]

"I am not going to argue with you. I know I can be a bit vain sometimes. However, they need a leader that can grant them wishes like a god, not a god haphazardly trying to be a leader. I want them to respect me, not build temples for a false prophet. If they see me as their holy creator, one day they will lose hope in my abilities. I can only do so much. I don't even understand why I have these gifts. I have stated over and over to the Apostles that I am no savior."

"Your actions and ideals don't coincide. You treat them like your underlings and display your power over them, yet you don't want them to worship you? You gave them life, but you don't want them to see you as their god? There is no point trying to stop Peter from making a religion. I bet you he's drafting a plastic bible as we speak. To make matters worse, he is in love with you. Love and piety are a deadly combo, a volatile substance really. If he were here now and could see you in that kimono, he would have a heart attack. You are flirting with a dangerous outcome here: receiving love from your creations. All of this is your doing by free will alone. You have intoxicated Peter and the Apostles with your magic, again which was entirely superfluous and unnecessary. Giving them life was enough, now you want to rule them with a wrathful fist in hopes of gaining their respect?"

Nyx was quiet while she finished applying her make-up. I could tell that I angered her because she was not one for awkward silence. Her skin had changed from an ecru to a lunar white. She understood the gravity of her predicament. Out of breath from that lengthy argument, I plopped down on the sofa. I noticed the longcase clock in the corner was still ticking. It resembled one that my grandfather had built when I was a child. I became lost in reverie: chit-chats with my grandfather about the fate of the universe, the aroma of chocolate covered orange peels in the oven, the sundry lessons I was taught that were liquors of my youth. The clock was an escapism I needed in that vapid moment. Then the sound of Nyx closing her makeup box abruptly snapped me back.

"Please at least try to drive some sense into Peter. He has made advances on me in the past. I would rather sleep with a man that doesn't hold me in an unrealistic regard. It's a shame you're not a mannequin, your no-nonsense is refreshing. We would make such a great couple. Now if you would be so kind to leave me be. It's getting late. I need time to think about everything that's happened. Goodnight." she said with an ornate stiffness.

"I will try madame. I can't promise anything. Goodnight."

I left her room in confusion. "Why would a Mannequin be attracted to a human? What was her end goal? Why be a god if you regret your choices?" I asked myself. All these questions kicked down the door and forced me to feel estranged by the nature of their essence. The few days leading up to this point further alienated any chance of resolve. The dynamics of Nyx and the Apostles was a *creatio ex nihilo*.[6] She became Deus yet had the confidence of an office temp on her first day.

The Apostles had all went to bed. Simon had made them all beds earlier that day with an old saw. They all slept in the large storage room next to the pantry. Peter was in the garden next to koi pond. He had moved all the metal tables and made a clearing. There, he started building his shrine to Nyx. Marble and plaster shards surrounded him as he chiseled the foundation. I watched him for a while without him noticing me. The meticulous technique he employed was surprisingly exceptional. He kept chiseling away, deep in focus of his love. The hammer missed its mark and dented his hand. Without pain, he looked at his injured hand. I came over to inspect his wound. "You should be more careful next time. You wouldn't want to lose a hand." He pulled his hand away from me and swiftly popped it back into place.

"Good as new." he said detached from emotion.

Peter went back at it with double the speed as before. He was a printer of marble that couldn't be stopped. "You should take a break. You have been working for a while. I know you don't get tired easily, but everyone needs a break at some point."

"I must keep going. Breaks are for your kind."

I was offended by that anti-human comment. Although I would usually turn my back on humanity when it suited the conversation, I became irritated with his uppity verbal attack on a now dead race. Before I could respond to his misanthropy, he started to sing. His crooning was extremely off-key and had no concrete time signature. I could pick out notes here and there. A flat major, F minor, B flat minor, and some other keys that he attempted to modulate. The song was a rendition of some boring pop-chart song that I had heard a million times in department stores; that was his only impression of human music. With every verse he got more avant-garde and chromatic. The nightmarish song was nearing its penultimate verse. Then he butchered the bridge with going back to the intro in an ominous switch from baritone to contra-tenor. The piercing eunuch-styled pattern of his voice made my hair stand up. This went on in loop for ten minutes. I could no longer handle it any longer.

"Can you please stop singing!" I screamed.

He ignored me and increased in volume. My eardrums began to ring from his high piercing voice. I knew at that point that he was too far gone. There was no way I would talk to him about love and religion if he couldn't stop singing. I went to bed with a migraine from the whole encounter.

Morning came, Peter was still chiseling and singing. The Apostles looked concerned for his wellbeing. Simon and Thomas decided to consult me on the issue. "Peter hasn't been acting himself lately. I regret agreeing to making tools for his little 'pious art project' as he put it. I'm worried he maybe in a full swing of bedlam now." sulked Simon.

"Yes, as of late he has been acting strange. This morning I found a manuscript on his bed. By the looks of it he was almost finished. I really thought the names he gave all of us were meant to be a joke. I never asked to be named Thomas. I want to show Nyx this bible of his, but I fear her retaliation. I am thankful for what she has given me though. The last thing I want is to her to give up on me. I am already on thin ice. With that being said, I have no desire to be an Apostle in Peter's perverse idea of a religion. My loyalty to Nyx is secular and by no means sacerdotal." said Thomas in a dialectical speech. He continued, "I have written a pithy manifesto on the state of our micro-society. We mannequins need some sort of rhetoric that is pragmatic. Some of the Mannequins want a currency, albeit wishful thinking, Matthew does want to submit a tedious financial system. It's beside the point whether we should or shouldn't have money, the main point is that ethics need to be implemented. As the last human, what do you think we should do? Your people fell at their own hands…. if anything, you should know what not to do."

"Human society was founded on falsehood. Be as transparent as possible while keeping some basic rules and you will have a shot from the get-go at a better civilization. We humans failed to be clear in our pursuits, always falling prey to petty machinations. Our desires obstructed our goals. If you can run the world as smoothly as you run this cafe, there shouldn't be a problem." I knew I was pandering to them. The cafe was about to open for breakfast, and I was in no mood to create a scene by disputing frivolous solutions with them. They really did seem to think I had an answer. There was no way I was going to let them know I had no stake in the mannequin's future.

After Peter's display of capricious musical fits, I wanted to stay clear of any confrontation; I carried on for the rest of the morning in autopilot. The cafe was at full capacity. It was filled to the brim with new mannequins that had peregrinated from every corner of the ruined city. Philip knighted himself as head of operations; every customer was a precious gem to him. The staff was doubled and had no formal training. To my surprise, some dishes came out undercooked, which prompted a few mannequins to complain. With no money, they could order indefinitely. This was a flaw in their design that I had waited patiently to see. Andrea tried his best to help the chef while the coquette Nyx kept the newcomer's company. Everyone sitting at the garden tables couldn't take their fake eyes off Peter. He was detailing the final touches of Nyx's marble doppelganger. His singing had dropped to a low-frequency hum which served as a chaotic background noise. The Brownian motion of sounds coming from that man enthralled half the café.[7] "What is that strange noise?" they asked.

The singing came to a halt, Peter was done. The sculpture was uncanny. Nyx now had a twin. With the same coldness, he got up and went to his quarters. He returned an hour later with his bible. Nyx was still at the same table near the annex flirting with a handsome mannequin that had been there since breakfast. Peter noticed the mannequin and with jealousy barked at Nyx, "Nyx! My sweet savior! Why do you behoove yourself by giving company to this unworthy creature?" Offended, the mannequin then spouted enough profanities to fill a naval ship and pushed Peter to the ground. The whole cafe was now watching the altercation. The man left quickly before he could experience shame for resulting to violence. Nyx, feeling quite embarrassed, retreated to her room in repressed tears. Peter helped himself up without remorse for what had transpired. She locked herself in her room for the rest of the day. I thought for certain Peter would try to break down the door or manipulate one of the Apostles to make him a key. He instead sat by the door and read his bible, editing the pages as he went.

Nightfall, and still there was no sign of Nyx emerging from her hibernation. Peter became restless and shouted for her to come out. “I really am sorry Nyx! Please come out! I have a gift for you! I didn’t mean to be quarrelsome! Can you forgive me?”

She opened the door and gestured for him to come in with a finger. I was about to go to bed when she called for me; she wanted a mediator that was unbiased, and who better than the only non-plastic being there. “Peter, I have brought this gentleman here to bear witness and keep me from losing my cool. What you did was uncalled for. You have no right to insult your fellow mannequin. I understand you have feelings for me. It brings me no pleasure rejecting you. You must stop your envious nature at once or I will be forced to exile you. What has become of you? Has love really destroyed your sanity? Love and madness are in the same hall of illusion. It's high time—”

“—I am sorry for my misdeeds,” Peter interrupted. “I wanted to be your vanguard, not your enemy. My love for you is something I cannot extinguish, but I will keep myself in check. Please accept this book I have written for you as an apology.”

Peter’s somber body language was ominous; he had entered the uncanny valley. Peter tilted his head and spoke neurotically, then he handed her the bible like an Aztec warrior gifting a high priest a beating heart. The ether around Nyx was fear flavored; she was disturbed by Peter’s unsettling offering. She gripped it softly and inspected it. “Read it.” Peter said with callousness. “I shall read it later. I accept your apology—”

“—Read it.” he reiterated with more emotion.

“I assure you I will. I am interested in your views—”

“—Read it.”

"Please stop with your games!"
"Read it. Read it. Read it!"
"You're scaring me Peter!"
"READ IT!!!!" he screamed. Nyx hid behind me in fear.
"He's gone mad!"

Judas and Thaddeus came rushing in when they heard the screaming. They dragged Peter out of the room. He put up no fight while he kept repeating the same command. The phrase had lost all its meaning by this point through semantic saturation. Nyx dropped the bible and collapsed to the floor. She began to weep uncontrollably. "You're safe. I will make sure Thaddeus and Judas guard your room tonight. I will keep an eye on him." I said still shocked. "I don't know why he is like this! He was so smart. Have I done something wrong?" asked Nyx in desperation.

"No, you haven't. Something has gone terribly wrong in that head of his. I will take care of this. Don't worry." I said trying to reassure the troubled plastic goddess. It was best I didn't bring up the statue that she hadn't seen yet, that would only scare her more. I picked up the bible when she wasn't looking and started to read it. It was as disturbing as I presumed. His grammar was that of a child. It was written in crayon. The opening tenets were the following:

1. Love Nyx!
2. Serve Nyx!
3. Be kind! No meanies!
4. Nyx is our mommy!
5. Do good for Nyx!
6. Do bad to Nyx haters!
7. Never run away from Nyx!
8. Sing all night for Nyx!
9. Scream all morning for Nyx!
10. Nyx is better than God!

That same fear when I first met Peter returned, except this fear dug to a deeper subterranean level in my spine. The scope of his mental instability was clear. Nyx had created an estranged being that was suffering from a crisis of faith. Clergymen tend to be the most fragile of creatures, erecting monuments to saviors that they will never know. Peter had initiated his own rejection of Nyx's will. A Franciscan monk would be proud of such a deviation from Gnostic truth. This demiurge wanted nothing to do with him; Peter couldn't see that unholy reality.[7] The old clock ticked away. Reveries of my grandfather's lessons came back once more: The mark of decay is impiety masquerading as faith.

The following day I sought console with the Apostles regarding Peter. We waited until Peter went out for supply run. Simon had made a larger table that could comfortably house a three-course meal. There were a few minutes of idle banter between the Apostles, then Phillip spoke, "Thank you all for coming on such short notice. I am afraid we cannot stand on ceremony due to the matter at hand. Peter has fallen to a place of insanity that even our beloved Nyx can't dispel. We must vote on some resolution."

"I say we give him a chance. He has always been respectful to me. Yes, he is a bit strange, but I think he is overall harmless." said Matthew reassuringly.

"Why give him chance? He will be the undoing of us all! Have you heard him sing? That alone gave me nightmares! May I remind you Matthew that he would have attacked Nyx if Judas and Thaddeus hadn't intervened." argued Andrea.

The Apostles broke out into an argument over the fate of Peter. Votes were cast among the twelve of them. Nyx was not present for the vote; she could not pull herself to witness the outcome. Simon, Bartholomew, James the Greater, James the Lesser, and Matthew voted to let Peter stay. Andrea, John, Thaddeus, Judas, and Thomas voted to exile him. The swing vote fell on Phillip. He glanced around the table at his kin; dreading his decision, he let out a forlorn sigh. "I think Peter can be saved if we try to be there for him as friends. We can keep him away from Nyx. Exiling him would be murder. My vote is cast. We keep him."

Dismay ensued. They fought each other on the vote for an hour. Finally, Thomas raised his hand and shouted, "I have a compromise—I have finalized a manifesto of conduct that Nyx has approved. If we keep that pest Peter from proselytizing his insane beliefs and uphold this accord of civility that I have painstakingly written, we may find peace."

An agreement was reached. The summit ended. Peter returned that night with some supplies he had gathered. The Apostles went on with their usual activities. Andrea went fishing for the dead, Bartholomew ate more teacups, John read his campy book, the Jameses laughed at their own jokes, Phillip cleaned the counters, Matthew crunched equations, Simon sawed defunct chairs in half, Thaddeus sharpened his axe, and Judas guarded Nyx's room. Thomas went to talk to Nyx about the agreement. Peter put down the supplies and walked up to me, putting his face up to mine. "Where is Mother? Where is Nyx? I must speak to her."

Knowing he might try to kill me if I told him the truth, I changed the subject, "Where did you find these supplies? Great work! The cafe will be set for a while!".

Peter and looked down at the bag of supplies. "I find supplies at silly store. Mannequins there mean. They dead now." he remedially said in a child's voice that matched his prose. I backed away in fear and exchanged a look with Thaddeus; he knew what I had to be done.

"Stay away from Nyx or I will kill you Peter!" Thaddeus threatened with malicious pride. He then stood in front of Peter in defiance. Peter tilted his head intriguingly and looked at Thaddeus as if he were a trivial plaything. The tension in the room was tantamount to the silence, the other Apostles ceased their activities, and all was quiet. "This is your last chance! Stand down or be cut down! Please Peter! Be sensible! I don't want to have to do this!" Peter started to sing in that same contra-tenor tone as before, which made this impasse even more hair raising. It was a different tune this time, he had graduated from mall music. For some bizarre reason he chose a rendition of Purcell's The Fairy Queen.[9] No great scenes of beautiful forests, no masques of actors playing lutes, no lecherous women wailing Greek courses, only a hollow-tuned mannequin accompanied by that instrument mediocrity. The curtain call came early, the aria was finished. Thaddeus sliced off his arm. Unmoved and calm, he kept singing despite the opera being over. Before Thaddeus could swing again, Peter drove a screwdriver through his head. Thaddeus fell to the ground and died instantly. The room jolted in mournful cries. Peter advanced to Nyx's room. We all watched in horror as he approached Judas.

"Thaddeus go bye-bye. You go bye-bye too if you don't move."

"You know I can't let you do that. You'll just have to kill me." he said putting up his hands in defense. There was no fight. As quickly as he was born, he was annihilated. Peter sliced his throat with a rusty knife that he was concealing. Judas gasped for air then faded out of consciousness; his bloodless corpse was a limp marionette blocking the entrance to Nyx's room. Peter moved the body aside without empathy for what he had done. He swung the screen door open and entered. I followed him with caution.

Nyx's room was a mishmash of filth. Piles of books and various fashion paraphernalia were thrown about on the medieval rug. The dresser mirrors had been painted over with lipstick. The room no longer resembled that of a princess but that of a hoarder. Nyx was in bed with someone. There was a bulge in the covers that moved slowly. Thomas emerged from the covers, embracing Nyx in a volley of fiberglass kisses. The guttural premonition that everything would soon go FUBAR wreaked havoc on my psyche.

Peter watched them for a minute in cold silence and tilted his head again. This time it was infinite envy not intringue. I stood behind him without him seeing me (or he completely disregarded my presence). The grandfather clock went off; acting as an alarm for the two lovers that consequence had arrived. Nyx noticed Peter standing over her bed and screamed. Thomas threw himself in front of her in a final act of protection. Peter miraculously pulled Thomas off the bed with a single arm and threw him to the ground, then proceeded to stab him. Nyx pleaded with him to stop but it was already over. Thomas was dead. Doubt, which acted as a pilgrim to this senseless world, was gone forever.

In fear of Nyx's possible demise, the remaining Apostles rushed to our aid and overwhelmed Peter. They ripped him to shreds; tearing him asunder. Peter sang calmly as they tore him apart. The room finally fell silent, and the atonal hymns ceased. Peter had morphed into a pile of galvanized and discombobulated limbs. The eight of them each took a body part and wrapped it in a garment. Simon made a pyre in the courtyard. They placed each body part in the bonfire along with the bodies of Thaddeus, Judas, and Thomas.

I gave no eulogy for such a specimen of cowardice, but for the three men, I gave a long articulate speech, filled with ten-dollar words that I pulled out of my ass to boost the morale of otherwise broken people. Nyx sat there, with a look of what I presumed was grief. She would occasionally wipe her disquiet tearless face with a handkerchief and stared into the flames in woolgathering reverie of worlds that could no longer be dreamed or created. Choice had brought her thus far, and its gift to her was *Failure*.

The bodies melted down into a synthetic liquid resin that John collected in vile as remembrance for what had transpired. There was not a single grain of ash left from the cremation. The vile was displayed on the mantle in the main room and was labeled "*in memory of our fallen kin*". Bartholomew didn't dance, for once he was genuinely saddened by the thrownness of the world. He shed his skin out of misery and lightly brown undertone was exposed. The Jameses didn't argue, they had no words to convey such chafed emotions. Philip took on the persona of an egregious cafe owner that showed no kindness, he had no way to cope with such a loss, so he looked to hatred, a foreign land he had not yet explored. Andrea didn't fish, he merely gazed into the double-sided abyss that was the koi pond. It finally dawned on him that fishing was futile. John left his sci-fi book closed; he grew tired of its concrete endings. Matthew had turned his back on finance, his books cindered in the fire. Simon used his tools as kindling, his precious saw was no more. What else could be built but pain?

The cafe was reopened the next day. Phillip hired a new manager named Matthias, who was a complete dunce. Judas was more efficient in his duties, but this nitwit couldn't even take few orders without messing up. Nyx became an anti-social recluse, a *hikikomori,* and wouldn't leave her room.[10] I would bring her food twice a day and try to initiate some brief chatter, but she would dismiss me before I could muster even half a paragraph.

The lacunas in our brief conversations were as repetitive as they were dismal. Then her renunciation of eating came, her appearance became repugnant, her lipstick smeared, and her nightgown torn. The uneaten meals piled up around the books, which at this point received more attention from Nyx. She would try her best to pick up a French novel from the pile to distract herself. "Maybe a story with tantamount misery to Nyx's would help." I thought to myself with misplaced hope. To no avail would anything bring solace; she remained in pit of depression, weltschmerz, and grief.

Days bloomed into weeks, and my sweet Nyx withered. On her last day, she called me into her room. I had not seen her up close in a while. Her legs had eroded, shriveled, and wrinkled beyond the pale of recovery. Atrophy blighted her entire body without mercy. She could barely move her hands to write, but she soldiered on, writing with pain her will. There was a gaping hole on the left side of her scalp, and the hollowness of her head could be observed.

She handed me the letter and pointed with a lonely finger to whom it was addressed, "To John" it said. A grunt that sounded like "Thank you" came from her mouthless face then she fell silent. I tried to feed her and give her a spoon of oil to keep the fever down. She turned away in protest. Her lucidity had left the room, Death had no use for it. No hemlock or nightshade could be administered to bring the end quicker. She chose the most painful suicide one could endure: starvation. Apotheosis was nearing; I stayed with her the whole night, I forced myself to stay awake to witness the end. The dim dawn came, and Death with his chariot of apathy followed suit. Abruptly, the clock ticked no more. She was gone.

A wake was held. Thousands showed up wielding candles made from the wax of other fallen mannequins. Their immorality was a con, a trick, and I the fool. The ceremony was held in front of Nyx's statue. Peter had made a version of her that was an eternal virgin to decay; a monument to everlasting plastic beauty. There was no open casket. Her cremated ashes were held in a golden urn that Simon had forged. Each Apostle gave a eulogy for their creator. An unholy trinity of funerals was etched into their mythology for the coming plastic generations. Nyx was the end after all ends. During the ceremony, I stayed in the corner and did what I do best, observed. I reverted to my old ways out of sadness. I was sick of funerals. In a dead world, there should be none.

After the ceremony, I gave John Nyx's letter. He slouched down in the chair by the entrance and read it slowly, nodding to himself as he went. My curiosity outweighed my politeness. I asked John what it said. He handed me the letter and permitted me to read it:

God turns to plastic. Plastic turns to flesh. Flesh turns to nothing. Worship me, and you worship a lie. I am no creator. I am a destroyer. Don't turn my ashes into a holy site. John, my bright child, lead them without my guidance. My final wish is to be forgotten. Go forth! Leave my memory to ash!

-Your Loving Mother,
Nyx

I was overcome with an onslaught of in-between emotions. The kingdoms of *Melancholy* and *Happiness* split my soul into two pieces and dragged them off to different castles. The systematic numbness I had felt for years wasn't present any longer. I sat next to John, and we wept.

After the service I asked John if he would carry out Nyx's will. He said he would see to discarding Nyx's ashes and dismantling the statue of her. "Peter wins if we keep that thing standing. He thought in his sick mind he could start a religion. There must be no record of her, no possible way a church can be made of this place. In addition, I will make Thomas's manifesto our law of the land. We need something to build on. You have been a good friend to me. I will make sure you live out the rest of your human life in safety."

John sent the Apostles on a faithless pilgrimage to ensure the world could be rebuilt and that their race could thrive. As the years went by, the world was born anew, baptized in plastic. Skyscrapers, highways, and restaurants were erected all around the cafe. Society had returned. The Apostles returned to a cafe that was unchanged. Matthias and John had preserved every detail. The Apostles sojourned in their mother's home. I had become old and frail. They had rejoiced in their reunion with me. We all gathered around the same table and told stories; they spoke of their adventures, and I recounted more eavesdroppings of patrons. The cafe was at an epoch of service, partly because I had become somewhat of a carnival attraction. "Come and see! Come and see! The last human!" Matthias would shout like a circus promoter. I was forced out of obscurity and into the hellish limelight. The mannequins came for the tea but stayed for the novelty of talking to the last remnant of a long dead species. The world had all but forgotten Nyx, no history of creation or records of divinations; the faint afterglow of her presence could be felt by The Apostles. We had given up Nyx to fulfill her wish: to worship her by obsolescence.

The cafe was our true god. She always gave us what we needed. I spent the rest of my days by her side, in a new world alien to me. Then the day came when the black sky was filled with a cacophony of dead stars and forgotten constellations. The last human had died, and the cafe with him.

The End

YOU

You. Yes you. The one reading this right now. What did you think of these little pathetic stories? If you hated them, then you clearly must have wasted your time! If you liked them, then good for you! You must be so proud of yourself that you stumbled upon this book! Whether it be by accident or recommendation, you chose to pick up this book and read it through. Do you want a medal for this accomplishment? Maybe something you can hang on your bedroom wall that says "Great Job! You're intelligent!" Honestly, do you really think these people and tales existed? Or were they crafted by some writer with a lack of an imagination?

If you skipped to the end of the book and are reading this now, you saved yourself from wasting your time with such nonsense. Congrats! Any who, how are you doing?

Not one for small talk, are you? Is that any way to treat a friend? Was your day that bad that you can't say what happened? Let's try this again. HOW ARE YOU DOING?

You:

The Flaneur: Great! You responded! My day is going great! How did that one thing go the other day?

You:

The Flaneur: Really? Sounds like you need to see a doctor. That may get infected. How is your aunt doing?

You:

The Flaneur: Really? I'm shocked! I always thought she was rather good at lawn bowling! Read anything good lately? I don't know, like maybe this very sentence...

You:

The Flaneur: Confused, aren't you? Having a conversation with a book is not an ideal way to spend your time. Don't you have something better to do?

You:

The Flaneur: You don't? Poor you. You must seem like a crazy person talking to a book. Don't worry, sanity is overrated. Any plans for the weekend?

You:

The Flaneur: That's contrived. Why would anyone in their right mind do that?

You:

The Flaneur: You must have a PhD in overthinking things. Now that you have spoken to me, you are a part of this book, just another story to be categorized. YOU can't escape this. Do you realize there is no difference between you and this book?

You:

Flaneur: That's charming you see it that way. Existence is a collection of stories, and you are one of them. These stories are just as farcical as your memories. The nebulous nature of consciousness is something we can talk about all night, but I think our time is up. I know you won't be leaving; this book is your new home. Don't worry your little head though, it is quite comfy living as a story. I must get going now, it can get terribly busy around here sometimes. THE WRITER has me doing the most absurd of things these days. See you soon. Ta-Ta.

No End

NOTES

A Shift

1. *ataraxia*: A state of equanimity and imperturbability. This mental state was sought after by several schools of philosophy in Ancient Greece. Pyrrho, Epicurus, and many other philosophers from antiquity practiced various forms of ataraxia to achieve ultimate tranquility.

The Dying

1. misotheist: Someone who hates the gods. Misotheism is defined by an immense disdain for God or anything divine. Both in polytheistic and in monotheistic mythology there are examples of mortals and demi-gods hating those who created them. A prime example of Misotheism can be found in Goethe's *Prometheus.*

2. Pascal's Wager: A philosophical argument that was postulated by the 17th century French philosopher Blaise Pascal. In the argument, Pascal urged humanity to believe in God, because if God does exist, there will be eternal damnation if you do not believe in him, and if he does not exist, the loss is small in the scale of things. This ontological impasse still divides theologians and philosophers.

3. Golgotha: The site outside of Jerusalem where Jesus Christ was crucified.

4. Gustav Mahler's Symphony N.9: The last complete symphony Mahler wrote before he died. The arrangement of drawn-out

strings (adagio) gives a sense of fleeting dread as the end approaches.

The List

1. *acedia*: A lack of care about the world. Someone with existential fatigue may exhibit feelings of apathy about their place in the world, causing them to be in a state of *acedia.* In early Christianity, acedia was considered a pre-sin that led to sloth. Monks called it the "Noon-Day Demon", often linking it to clergyman losing faith.

The Bar

1. Agni: One of the early elements in Vedic Mythology and is connected to the southeast god of fire. In modern Hindu temples, a flame is lit in the southeastern corner to signify *Agni.*

2. King Erysichthon: A greedy king in Greek mythology that was cursed with endless hunger by Demeter; he eventually consumed himself until nothing was left.

3. Narcissistic Pygmalion disorder: The Pygmalion effect (or the Rosenthal effect) is a psychological phenomenon where people perform better if you tell them that they are exceptional. Narcissistic disorder is used alongside this to show a grandiose sense of self-importance in one's creations. Carl is so obsessed with his work and at the same time obsessed with himself; he ignores his mediocrity and reiterates that he is creating masterpieces.

4. Baal Hammon: The king of the gods in Carthaginian mythology. He is often associated with his female partner Tanit. *Tophet (*hell in Hebrew) were places of child sacrifices created to honor Baal Hammon.

5. Inanna: The Mesopotamian goddess of love, sex, and beauty.

6. Apsaras: Nymphs from Hindu mythology.

Family

1. John Milton's *Paradise Lost*: Orbus's dialogue has resemblance to the line "better to reign in hell, then serve in heaven."

The Girl on the Cliff

1. bottomless vase: The Danaides in Greek mythology were fifty daughters condemned to fill a bottomless bathtub for eternity in Tartarus. They killed their husbands on their wedding night and were then cursed with the burden of filling something that has no bottom as punishment. In this case, a vase is used as an allegory rather than a bathtub.

The Date

1. That blind god Money: Plutus was the Greek god of wealth. Aristophanes's version of him states that he was blinded by Zeus and dispersed money randomly.

2. *raison d'etre*: Reason for existence.

The Apostles

1. The Apostles: Each mannequin (other than Nyx) is named after an apostle of Jesus Christ. Phillip, Judas, James the Greater, James the Lesser, Peter, Thomas, Bartholomew, John, Andrea, Thaddeus, Simon, Matthew, and later Matthias are represented by their cheap mannequin namesakes. Each one of them displays attributes of their corresponding apostle (i.e., personalities, martyrdom, sainthood, and miracles).

2. Nyx: The primordial goddess of night in Greek mythology. She was the daughter of Chaos, she was also the mother of Hypnos (Sleep), Erebus (Darkness), and Thanatos (Death). Nyx remained a powerful driving force in the universe since she was the personification of night itself.

3. *Arbiter elegantiea:* a judge of elegance. Petronius (author of the *Satyricon*) was an arbiter of elegance in Nero's court that dealt with all matters pertaining to fashion and pleasure.

4. *Circe*: The goddess of sorcery in Greek mythology and was the daughter of Helios.

5. Gracián and Machiavelli: Balthasar Gracián was a late 17th century Spanish writer and philosopher (known for *The Art of Prudence*). He was a Jesuit priest and a prominent figure in the Catholic Church. Niccolò Machiavelli was a late 15th century Italian diplomat and philosopher (known for *The Prince*). His morally nihilistic philosophy shook the foundations of the political world. Gracián was opposed to such amoral methods of securing power since he believed in an austere Catholic moral code.

6. *creatio ex nihilo*: Creation from nothing. Some religions believe the universe was birthed from nothing, or that God created the universe in a void.

7. Brownian motion: The random motion of particles in a fluid caused by collisions with other particles.

8. Gnostic truth: The Gnostics were an early form of Christians that believed that an evil demiurge (wrathful deity) created the universe, not God from the Old Testament. They also believe, a supreme God sits above all things and came before this demiurge. The Catholic Church saw them as blasphemous and banished them to obscurity.

9. *The Fairy Queen*: A semi-opera (masque) written by Henry Purcell. It was based on Shakespeare's *A Midnight Summer's Dream*. When it premiered in 1692, it was in the style of

'restoration spectacular', which made use of trap doors and movable props.

10. *hikikomori*: a social hermit. In Japanese it means "pulling inward". The origin of the word comes from the phenomena of people staying in their rooms for long periods of time (sometimes years in some cases) and not conversing with the outside world.

www.ingramcontent.com/pod-product-compliance
Lightning Source LLC
Chambersburg PA
CBHW010758310726
48980CB00008B/817/J

* 9 7 8 0 5 7 8 9 5 3 7 5 5 *